PRAISE FC

"A battle cry for female rage and wild spirits, ... ll weaves a dark, grotesque story that leaves you questioning who the monsters really are: the vicious gods or the heartless men."

— CHESNEY INFALT, AUTHOR OF *THE MAGIC COLLECTOR*

"The Bone Drenched Woods is a dark and haunting tale full of twisted traditions, sharp teeth, and unsated desires. Hyacinth's story gripped me from the first page. A must-read!"

— LOGAN SPURGEON, AUTHOR OF *HINTERLAND*

"*The Bone Drenched Woods* is the kind of folk horror that crawls under your skin and takes root, forcing you to witness every gruesome moment. L.V. Russell once again does what she does best—slow-burn horror that won't let you go."

— CASSANDRA L. THOMPSON, AUTHOR OF *THE AGONY OF HER* AND *WELCOME TO MEADOWBROOK*

THE BONE DRENCHED
WOODS

THE BONE DRENCHED WOODS

L.V. RUSSELL

Quill &
Crow

THE BONE DRENCHED WOODS
BY L.V. RUSSELL
PUBLISHED BY QUILL & CROW PUBLISHING HOUSE

This book is a work of fiction. All incidents, dialogue, and characters, except for some well-known historical and public figures, are either products of the author's imagination or used in a fictitious manner. Any resemblance to actual persons, living or dead, or actual events is purely coincidental.

Cover/Interior Design by Fay Lane

Edited by Cassandra L. Thompson

Printed in the United States of America

ISBN: 978-1-958228-82-1

ISBN: 978-1-958228-81-4 (ebook)

Publisher's Website: www.quillandcrowpublishinghouse.com

This one is for the Crows

PUBLISHER'S NOTE

This book contains scenes of graphic violence, including graphic violence toward women. Please be advised.

CHAPTER ONE

T he sun shone bright on Hyacinth's seventeenth nameday, the heat of summer having bleached the color from the grass. The wildflowers for her hair were dry and dull, as brittle as the smile on her mother's face. Scraps of fabric hung from the long-limbed trees, sewn and hung by the women of the village, the sun at their backs as they made a patchwork of her life.

Wavering in the scarce breeze was a strip of her baby blanket, her first dress, the cardigan her grandma knitted when winter came. White silk fluttered in the middle, the pale pink ribbon stained from where Angus Bartleby had shoved her in the mud. Her best dress from her sacrament, the vows to her elders falling falsely from her tongue. She remembered them perfectly, recited with a smirk she was later beaten for.

Seventeen ragged flags, all tied by a rope woven by the menfolk. Space remained at the end, a vacant spot where scraps of her wedding gown would one day fly, bloodied and ruined.

She could almost feel the bonds of matrimony tighten around her, squeezing her like the ill-fitting corset her mother now forced her into. There was a comfort to her childhood village, a known order of things. There were the whispers at night between her sisters, soft laughter, and relief when they heard their father come home. She knew the voices of the village, the footsteps, the songs, the prayers and shouts, knew it all. She did not want to learn the sounds of somewhere new, paired off with one of the boys she once threw rocks at.

"Mind your tongue, Hyacinth," her mother said, lacing the stays of her dress, pulling them tight enough to catch her breath. Tight enough to choke the words from her. "Play nice, and maybe—*maybe* —we can have a spring wedding."

Hyacinth shifted, easing the boning from beneath her ribcage. "I am nice."

Fingers caught her chin, nails digging in. "You are a disgrace."

She remained there, caught in her mother's unflinching hold, wondering if there had been a time when the hand on her face had been tender, a loving caress, and not a warning. Her mother seldom showed any gentleness as though watching her eldest daughters vanish into the woods had stripped it from her.

Hyacinth remembered their pale faces, the blush of their skin drained and replaced with trepidation. She remembered the blood on their necks, dried in the summer sun, their ruined wedding gowns torn and added to the remains of their childhood, flapping sadly in the breeze. Perhaps she had been too young to understand they would not come home.

First went Heather, hands knotted with a lanky red-haired boy whose name Hyacinth never bothered to learn. Hyacinth had danced and laughed, and then her sister was gone, the tracks leading into the woods dry and cracked. The following year, Dilly was wed. Hyacinth did not dance or laugh. She watched the ruined silk be torn into strips and hung with a curled lip. No goodbyes passed her lips.

"How do we know the trees will not eat them?" she had asked her mother, peering into the shadows.

"Because your father cleared the paths," came her mother's tear-choked and trembling answer. "The Woodsmen made them safe.

Your sister has her carved bones, her circlet, and the carvings on her carriage. She is safe, I know it."

"You hope it," Hyacinth had whispered, knowing it was not the same thing, not even a little bit.

Blind faith did not come easily to Hyacinth, and though she did try, she found she could not soak in the words of the Elders. She wanted to—she *used* to want to. To close her eyes and whisper comforting words to make the monsters in the darkness seem less so. But they kept coming, and more prayers were uttered, more blood and bone spilled out over branches, over hewn earth. And still, they came.

"Will you miss me, Mother?" Hyacinth tilted her chin, slowly meeting the soft blue of her mother's eyes. They were so unlike hers, pretty and pale and lovely. "When I am taken elsewhere?"

"As I would miss all of my daughters."

"Would you let me choose?" Her path, her fate, her death.

The hand on her face dropped, and she was turned around. More flowers were added to her tangles, the wheat-colored curls remaining wild around her face no matter her mother's attempt to tame it.

"Mother?"

"I think not, Hyacinth."

Two of her sisters were wedded and sent far away to make new lives in new villages far from home. It was finally Hyacinth's turn. She would never see her family again. She would not come home.

"What if I do not wish to marry?" she asked, the words slipping past her tightened chest despite the bindings. "What then?"

Her mother turned then, sweeping the tears from her cheeks. "Do you know where they send those who do not follow our ways?"

Hyacinth glared back. "To the Teeth."

The word hung in the air between them.

"Sometimes, yes. Other times, they are put elsewhere."

Hyacinth shivered, realizing what she meant. In her tenth year, she had been taken, alongside the other children, to learn their futures should they decline to wed. To the Farm. Sometimes still, when Hyacinth closed her eyes, she could see them—the girls and boys who had refused the paths set out for them. She remembered the smell more clearly, so different from the rich, coppery tang of steaming blood over earth. It reminded her of spoiled meat, a different sort of rot. The wind carried that stench as Hyacinth and the other children were led to the clearing.

Stretches of tilled ground were abundant with maize and greens, golden stalks swaying in the soft breeze. It might have been beautiful, peaceful even, if not for the dead children standing above the stalks on small wooden platforms, their arms stretched wide over posts, fingers splayed out, flesh nibbled, bleeding, and raw. One thin, sharp-ended spike protruded from the gaping mouths as though it had grown there. Tongues lolled, fat and dry, cheeks once youthful lay hollow, cleaved apart, showing bone.

Hyacinth would never forget the smell of them, nor the sounds they made, left to a slow death. The crows would get them, piece by piece; they were not meant for the Teeth.

It left her with a sense of emptiness, a space she was told was meant for her faith. Though no matter the sermons she swallowed down, it remained hollow.

"A choice between where I am sent is no choice at all."

Her mother laughed, the sound unkind. "Then become a spinster, girl. Take your wild tendencies, your wicked mouth, your wanton soul, and go live alone. Let the woods have you. Let the trees eat you up."

"I would eat them first—"

The smack knocked her to her knees, her soft cotton dress dirtied by the floorboards. Hyacinth pressed a hand to her stinging cheek, refusing to swallow back the words. She let them echo, to soak into the timbres of the house for the Trees to hear.

"You dare!" her mother hissed. "You dare speak like that to me. My name day gift to you, my daughter, is to speak to no one of your blasphemy. Wipe the dirt from your knees, fix your smile, and for once, make me proud to call you my own."

Hyacinth had yet to see pride soften the hard lines of her mother's face. She still looked for it despite her quick tongue, her temper. But her mother looked at all her daughters with the same cold weariness, as though the Teeth took a piece of her with every child she sent through their shadows. All but little Elestren, who was still infant soft. Hyacinth's mother clung to the youngest Turning child as though soaking up the years she had left before all her daughters were gone.

So Hyacinth stood, her palms blackened from the fall. She brushed them down her legs, sweeping the dust from her skin and streaking them in black. Her hem was spotted in dirt, her shoes were scuffed, and some of the flowers had come loose from her hair. Yet she stood tall, her chin high, ready to make her mother oh so proud on her name day.

CHAPTER TWO

B eneath the remains of her childhood, long wooden tables stood upon the coarse grass, their tablecloths shining too white in the sun. Placed with care upon the pristine cloth were loaves of bread on platters, bowls of early fruit, and plates of jam tarts. They sat near tiered cakes laden with sweet strawberries and cream. Jugs of water were on offer beside decanters of summer wine. Around the food, and placed with care, were the antlered skulls of seventeen stags, their empty sockets holding the stems of wildflowers.

All for her. All for the woman she was meant to be. Flowers and bone, girl and woman, maiden and mother.

"Look at you!" Fingers entwined with hers, forcing her to spin on her tiptoes, her ruined dress flaring out from her legs. "You filthy heathen!"

Hyacinth pulled her hands free to slip into a low curtsy, her corset digging in deep. "Not nearly filthy enough, I fear."

Abelia Merrow curtsied back, her crow-black hair braided over her shoulders and tied at the ends with red ribbon. Freckles marked her skin, her nose reddened by the sun. With a crooked grin, she swiped at the dirt on Hyacinth's palms and streaked it across her cheeks.

"How do I look now?" Hyacinth asked, her face aching from her smile.

Abelia leaned in close, all honey soap and soil. "Like you will eat the trees."

Their friendship had been borne through snickers during sermons, the forced coughs to hide sacrilegious laughter. Abelia and her mother sat behind Hyacinth on the pews in the Drove, the wood cold and rough and uncomfortable. They traded glances, small smiles cut short when with a sharp dig of an elbow from Hyacinth's mother. Abelia was all wild eyes and dirty fingernails, her shadow already half in the woods, or so Hyacinth's mother told her. Hyacinth could smell the earthiness on Abelia like a perfume, and though she breathed it in deep, it was never quite enough. It sparked a longing in her, a different emptiness that was not there before, and she did not know how to fill it, quench it, forget it.

The entire village had come out to celebrate Hyacinth's name-day, dressed in their finest clothes to dance and feast with the sun high above them, feeling, for an afternoon, far away from the terror of the woods. Though the fear never quite left them, with the darkness only a walk away and the echoes that haunted the night so close. The trees stood watch around the village edge like silent sentries, their darkness a solid thing, broken only by one thin winding path that led through the stoic boughs.

A path her sisters had taken, dressed in white, wilted flowers in their hair, wilted smiles dying at their lips as they were sent on their way. They were blessed, she was told, and the woods would leave them alone. A path she would soon take.

Hyacinth took in the faces of her neighbors, the women who had wiped her scraped knees, mended her stockings, even gossiped behind her back. She watched the young girls. The way they chased the boys, their laughter high and piercing. She looked to Abelia, so much more wicked than she, and wondered who would feed the woods on her wedding day.

"Angus Bartleby has put his name in for your hand," Abelia said, snatching a tart from the table. "Reckon he'd quite like to muddy your skirts again."

Hyacinth stuffed a cake in her mouth, picking the strawberries from the others before devouring them, too. "I don't think I'd mind it this time."

"You like him?"

She licked the sugar from her fingers. "He's not the worst of a bad bunch."

She could wish for little more; to be sent off into the woods with a boy she had smiled with and joked with would not be the worst thing, she supposed. Love was laughable, and there was little use in it. She had watched too many friends be taken by the Teeth, scant remains left behind. Love was a forever opening wound, and grief its scarred tissue. She had built herself a thickness of skin, an armor against it all. Sometimes, she wished she felt more, but a tiny crack and she would peel open, all her thoughts and hopes and dreams spilling out where they could be seen. Her mother would have a fit.

"Who would be your first choice?"

You.

Hyacinth looked to the trees, into the darkness beyond. If she listened carefully, she imagined she heard the whispers, the cries, the half-wild keening of the crones. The heathens, the forgotten.

With jam-sticky fingers, she brushed a lock of Abelia's hair behind her ear, feeling the powdery grit of dirt embedded in the curl. Her cheeks were freckled with it, splashes of mud so faint they were hardly there at all, but Hyacinth saw. She could smell the moss on her, the sweetness of it, forbidden and raw. Abelia grinned, showing teeth.

"Who would you choose, Hyacinth?"

Hyacinth blinked, sucking down the scent of pine. "Myself."

Abelia pulled her close, sticky hands holding her tight. Her breath was warm and wood rot-sweet. She could taste the jam on her words.

"We could both go."

Into the woods, into the dark. Abelia would go with her, following those who had chosen a gaping maw over tied hands. And perhaps they would find they belonged there, wicked and hungry, their bones left alone, their souls left whole.

Hyacinth had long felt the rumbles in her bed, the sound of claws over earth. It filled her dreams, the sounds of the Teeth so deeply ingrained within her that she feared it had carved itself on her bones. If they strung her up and peeled back her skin, would they see? She was afraid, for she was no fool...but she was not nearly afraid enough.

She also heard the singing of the wild women from her bed, the echoes of high-pitched keening, followed by laughter. She had been told it was a wicked sound as she sat on the wooden pew beside her sisters. Wicked, evil, blasphemous. Worse than whores, those women who threw themselves to the Teeth, exposing their muddied flesh to ancient beings. But she would lie awake some nights, eyes straining against the dark, and listen. Her heart would still, and she heard the subtle thread of something calling to her. An outstretched hand, a grin, a dare. With her sisters slumbering around her, Hyacinth lay still, humming to herself.

"You would never have to leave the village," Abelia continued, a gleam in her apple-green eyes. "We wouldn't have to leave each other."

The small word balanced on the edge of Hyacinth's tongue, a quick acceptance dangling before she sucked it back. To marry and be sent away would be the safest choice, the only choice if her mother had her way. Dressed in her best gown, bones at her hip, hands tied with some boy she found almost tolerable. A slow death, she thought, but the woods... There were no promises with the Teeth, no certainty. The unknowing of it tempted her, drawing her in. To be undestined and free. A death of her own choosing if her life could not be.

"Are you not afraid?" Hyacinth asked, needing to share the worry she would not be enough for the trees. That all she was and ever would be was a girl with a wicked tongue and bones only good for hanging.

Abelia closed the space between them, lifting her arm to press her wrist to Hyacinth's mouth. Her skin was cold, the pulse beneath her lips thrumming.

"Can you taste that?" She pressed harder, knocking against Hyacinth's teeth. The saltiness of sweat slipped past her lips. "My fear is as slick as yours."

"When would we go?"

Abelia looked up over to the dancing crowd, to the villagers devouring the offerings the way the woods devoured theirs. "Tonight, Hyacinth. We go tonight."

So soon. There would be no time to think, to change her mind, to settle herself on a village boy and be sent into the trees. Hyacinth remembered the names of the couples who came through, journeying past the Teeth from their villages to hers. They always arrived so tired, so pale, their clothing dirty, their eyes wide. They shared tales of where they'd come from, and Hyacinth had huddled close, pushing past the others so she could hear, hungry for the stories.

One newly wedded couple came in after the sun had slipped below the treeline, wooden wheels clacking over earth. How the horse had continued to pull them along was a mystery, with its mane threaded with vine and rib cage scored open. Hyacinth could see its heart, wrapped in ivy, beating against the bone. The newly-weds fared little better, their bodies tangled together by roots that writhed against them, seeking to slip beneath the earth once more. Red soaked the bride's gown, still trickling out from the shredded bone where her head should have been. In her lap, cradled between her clenched fingers with broken, soil-dark nails, lay her bride-groom's head. He had smiled up at the stars, lips stretched so wide they had split up over his cheekbones. Seedlings grew in the cracks of flesh, tiny white petals damp and heavy with blood.

Even with the paths cleared, sometimes the Teeth still took.

Hyacinth had tried, copying her elder sisters in the way they sat and talked. The way they took tea with the other polite girls in the village. She mimicked their smiles, the delicate way they dabbed at their lips, the coy way they spoke with the boys, all doe-eyes and blushing cheeks.

She had tried it once with Angus, keeping her eyes low, her hands clasped in front of her, hair braided almost neatly down one shoulder. He had laughed at her, cheeks ruddy and tear-streaked, breath wheezing from his lungs. He had wept real tears when she curled her fingers and struck him sharply across his face.

Hyacinth stumbled over her words, a part of her wishing Abelia would take her forcefully by the hand and drag her to the shadows. She would give them up, her choices, for Abelia. Only for her.

"I am going tonight." Abelia chewed a dirty fingernail, spitting at Hyacinth's feet. "Stretch your arms out."

"Why?"

"Just do it."

Hyacinth reached out as far as she could, fingers tense, until her shoulders ached. "Now what?"

"I just wanted to see." Abelia walked around her, hands lightly brushing over her skin. "You would not suit The Farm."

Hyacinth snapped her arms down, holding herself. She had seen —they had all seen—the crow-picked remains of the unwed who had turned their backs on their village. A circle of them not much older than Hyacinth. Arms stretched out, necks pinned back, all hollowed eyes and rotting skin. Weathered bone deemed not good enough for the Teeth to eat.

"Fuck off." Hyacinth moved, wrist jarring back as Abelia caught hold of her. She could have wrenched it away, forced her into the mud, but the squeeze on her fingers halted her, rooted her to the earth.

"I am going, Hyacinth, whether or not you are with me."

With a soft, secretive smile, Abelia tangled her fingers in Hyacinth's, bright eyes meeting hers, waiting. A vulnerability slipped over Abelia's features, a flash of innocence shining behind the layers of dirt and heathen thoughts. If her face was a mirror, Hyacinth couldn't tell.

"I'll go with you," Hyacinth said at last, her thoughts drifting to the strung-up remains of the unwed with their gaping mouths and thoughtless skulls. They went to their posts, still breathing, their screams echoing across the treetops. She had heard it from one of the village girls that the Teeth sometimes stood and watched. She imagined dying on one of those posts, head pinned just so, catching sight of glinting eyes from the shadows, knowing they were hungry but not hungry enough.

She'd rather the skin be sloughed from her bones. It seemed quicker.

Abelia held her hand tight, and together, they slipped back into the gathering, their secret knotted between them. Hyacinth danced with the village boys and smiled respectively at the women who had baked the cakes and the men who worked the fields. She bowed her head toward the Elders with their bloodied masks hiding their faces, noting the disdain in their eyes. The way they looked at her, as though eager to see her gone or eaten...as long as she was far away from them.

She saved a smile for her mother, a wordless goodbye. She felt lighter, the choice made, her future destined by her and Abelia and no one else.

"You have dirt on your cheeks," her mother said, eyes narrowed.

"But none on my knees."

"Four boys have put their name forward for you, Hyacinth." She lifted a hand, sweeping the pale hair from Hyacinth's face, tucking it behind her ear with an unusual tenderness. "A miracle, really, thank the gods."

"And who will I marry, Mother?"

"I have not yet decided. I want to wait for your father to come home. I will discuss it with him."

"But not with me?"

"Do not be foolish, Hyacinth."

Don't be foolish, or wicked, or loud. Don't be brazen, wild, hopeful, hungry. Be pretty, be quiet, be good.

Obedient.

Her nameday gathering stretched on into the evening, the summer sun stretching out into dusk, spilling pink and orange over the darkening blue. As the shadows lengthened, the crowd drew in, dancing closer, arms linked. Wine flowed, and crumbs scattered to the ground for the dogs to snatch at. Hyacinth was passed around, hands on hers, smiles too close to her face, breath hot on her cheeks.

She grinned back, all teeth, her heart already deep in the woods.

CHAPTER THREE

T he room Hyacinth shared with her remaining sisters was
small, nestled high up in the eaves of their cottage. They
were close to the trees, the shadows of the boughs slipping
over the windows, stretching out across the floor. Their father was
a Woodsman tasked with clearing the pathways through the woods,
hanging the offerings, and carving the bones to dangle from the
branches. From her bed, Hyacinth heard them clacking in the
breeze. The homes of the Woodsmen stood close together, almost
touching, a perfect circle around the village. To keep them all safe,
a fence of prayers and fearful men.

Their father was in the woods now with the other Woodsmen,
keeping the path clear so the carriages could come and go, taking
Hyacinth's friends and neighbors away, and bringing new folk from
villages afar. It kept the villages strong, Hyacinth was told. Kept the
stories stronger. The woods let those carriages go and come, let the
Woodsmen work, as long as they were fed, as long as they were
never left hungry.

The Woodsmen would come back before dawn, dirty and weary,
with calloused hands and heavy eyes. Hyacinth had washed blood
from her father's clothes many times, some of it his own, most not.

She watched her mother stitch up his wounds, slices in his flesh where a branch or a root had torn through. His skin was a patch-work of scars, but he came home. Hyacinth was always thankful that he came home.

From their bedposts, a bundle of bones hung from a roughly woven string, tied tight with knotted strands of their hair. The legs of four hares were offered for the wood, caught by Hyacinth's father and skinned by her mother the day she slipped from the womb, howling and bloodied, the same as all her sisters. Red seeped into the wood grain, a few lines long since dried, almost black. A mark, along with the bones, that the beds were paid for. The wood given. It would stop the Teeth from slipping in and snatching them from their beds while they slept. Or so they were told.

"Are you excited, Hyacinth?" Briony said, lying back against her pillow, her brown hair spilling from her braid. The sun had caught on her cheeks, brightening the freckles there and staining her nose red. "To think you danced with your future husband today!"

"Gods help him." Celandine grinned at Hyacinth from her bed, pulling off her shoes to fling them into the trunk they shared. She had the dark hair of their mother, an ink-spill down her back.

Hyacinth smiled, comfortable in her sisters' welcome presence. Elestren sat nestled between her legs, her head of dark curls barely coming up to Hyacinth's chin. She still carried the scent of infancy, a sweetness Hyacinth would bottle if she could. Elestren would be the last to wed, and she would do it alone. There would be no sisters left to dance with, to calm her fears of leaving, to carve bones for her to wear on her travels. She wondered who her mother would pick, who she would tie to the youngest Turning and send off into the trees. Hyacinth would not watch her grow nor see the last moments of ignorance seep from her smile and bright eyes. It came for them all in the end. Hyacinth wanted to reach back, reclaim it, hold it tight. They were not born afraid.

"I am surprised I had four offers," Hyacinth said, scooping Elestren up in her arms. She smelled like soap, the lavender one kept for special occasions. "I had hoped I scared them all off."

"Well, some were obviously drawn to your wild ways, Cinthe." Briony pulled back the covers on the one empty bed, and together, they tucked their youngest sibling in tight. The blankets were brought up to Elestren's chin, the bones on the bedpost checked over and straightened. "I reckon they think they can tame you."

Celandine bit into her nails, spitting a jagged piece onto the floor. "Or break you." She caught Hyacinth's eye, the grin slipping into a tight smile. "Don't let them."

She was not yet as savage as Hyacinth, her untrusting eyes muted, concealed by a cowed head and hands clasped around her oak circlet. Though perhaps she was just better at hiding it from their mother.

"What would you have me do?" Hyacinth asked.

Celandine's eyes flicked to the window, to the dark, famished woods. She did not voice it, not beneath the eaves and beside the carved bones. Hyacinth wondered, when the time came, if Celandine would choose the echoes, the gathering blackness, the shrill song that spilled over into their dreams. If not, she wouldn't marry quietly. A part of her believed their mother would allow Celandine the choice denied to her. If only Hyacinth had been quieter, better, more respectful, burying the wickedness she wore too brazenly beneath her skin where it belonged, her mother would have been kinder to her. Locked away the distasteful parts of herself so she could become loveable.

"I have seen the way you look," Celandine said, fingers playing with the ribbons on her nightdress. "You stare out into the dark with eyes as big as the moon."

"Do I, now?"

"And stare at that Merrow girl like you would like to lick the dirt from her face."

"Hush your tongues," Briony hissed, fingers going to the carved oak pendant at her neck. "You'll tempt the evil closer."

Hyacinth stood, stepping on silent feet to where Briony sat with white fingers gripping her knitted blanket tight. "It would eat you first," she teased.

"It would not!"

"You're so pious, Bry." Celandine came up to the side of the bed, leaning close. "It would swallow you up and leave no room for us heathens."

"I'll tell Mama!"

"You would tell me what?"

Their mother had stolen up the stairs, soundless. Her hair was unbound, the shining black curling over her shoulders down to the curve of her waist. She had taken off her best dress, replacing it with her brown, woven one, the pockets deep enough to hold spare bones and a little knife for carving them. The other blades, the ones for skinning the hares, for slewing off the flesh of heretics, heathens—those blades hung above the kitchen window.

"I said a curse word, Mother," Hyacinth lied, threading her fingers through Briony's. "Shook my sister to the core, it did."

"You are a wicked child, Hyacinth Turning." Their mother walked to the far bed and placed a kiss on her youngest daughter's head. She pressed more to the foreheads of Celandine and Briony, her hands sweeping over their soft hair. She paused before Hyacinth, then knelt in front of her, drawing her close to her chest. "You are a wicked, wicked girl."

"There are worse things to be," Hyacinth said into the warmth of her mother, to the echo of her heartbeat.

A kiss was pressed to her cheek, words gentle in her ear. Sad and resigned. "Not here, my daughter. Never here."

Night slipped over the house in a creeping quiet. One candle burned on the nightstand, creating fingers of shadow that stretched out as though to peer beneath the bedcovers to check if the sleepers in their beds were truly sleeping. Its lone flame kept the pitch from devouring the room completely.

Hyacinth heard breathy snores coming from Briony, mingling

with the gentle sounds of the others. She had waited for the house to settle, for her mother to douse the fire and light the lantern hanging from the porch for when their father returned. She listened for the creak of the stairs, for her mother's footsteps as she went to bed alone.

With the house asleep, Hyacinth slipped from her bed and pulled on her boots. She reached for her cloak, the good one with the sheepskin lining, and made to steal from her room. She felt it like an echo inside her, the place where the goodness of her heart should beat. It was longing and curiosity, a nerve stoked raw. Her heart thrummed with the chorus of the wild ones. She was as hungry as the oaks, as those beneath.

"Don't go." Briony was awake, her eyes wide and fearful. "Please, don't go."

"Hush!" Hyacinth hissed the word, fearing the lashing if caught out of bed. It might have been worse than a lashing if caught out of bed with her boots and cloak on. Would her mother send her to the gallows? Or beat the sin from her away in front of the damning eyes of the Elders? Hyacinth had seen families point fingers at their own to save their necks, had seen flames lick flesh clean from the bone with the approval of mothers, fathers, husbands, and wives.

Hyacinth leaned closer, her teeth close to Briony's cheek. "Or I'll drag you with me."

"I'll scream," Briony whispered back, blanket clutched tight.

"Then I will run." Hyacinth moved so close to her sister that their noses touched. "I will run into the night, and no one will catch me. I will be welcomed into the shadows, and I will tell them why I ran. They will come for you, Briony Turning. I will make sure of it. No pretty amulet will be enough to save your soul."

Tears slipped down her freckled cheeks, but Briony said nothing. Hyacinth watched as she pulled her blankets up higher, nearly covering her head. She looked up, meeting Celindine's dark gaze. Her other sister smiled, saying nothing.

"Come with me," Hyacinth mouthed the words, her hand stretched out.

The smile slipped from Celindine's lips, and she shook her head.

Hyacinth withdrew her hand, having expected the answer. Then she withdrew in haste, skipping over the steps she knew would creak. She grabbed an apple and some hard rolls and shoved them into her pockets, not knowing what food lay beyond the village. With one hand already on the door, she turned and quickly snatched up her mother's skinning knife from where it hung over the window.

The night air caressed her cheeks with the subtle chill of summer's end. She kept close to the houses, their lanterns swinging back and forth on their hooks like beacons in the dark. The grass was damp with dew underfoot, and a low mist curled around Hyacinth's ankles, almost guiding her, pulling her toward the trees. She paused as silence surrounded her, the branches still. There was no song on the breeze, nothing to call her on. If she turned back, no one but her sisters would know how she had slipped out, braved the edges of the woods, and tempted the Teeth. She could return to her bed, to her warm woven blankets with the rattle of carved bones at her feet, and be safe.

Though not free.

"Are you ready?" Abelia clutched her hand, slipping through the shadows like a wraith. She was grinning, her smile a wild slash of her lips.

Hyacinth found herself smiling back, reaching for the wilding in her and tethering it. Their fingers interlocked, holding tight as though they were but one, one wicked soul rooted in two.

They listened, standing before the dark wooded abyss. The tables from the party were still up, lying empty under the moon. The scent of sun-scorched grass and spilled wine was everywhere: a stain, a memory, a promise Hyacinth was forced to make with no intention of ever keeping. No one had asked. Finally, a song drifted across the bare tables, clinging to the wind. A piercing cry, a savage call, a beacon for those away from the trees. It thrilled her, drowning out all thoughts of warm blankets and whispered sins, of sermons and men in masks.

"Come on!" Abelia tugged her on, fingers squeezing tight. "Don't look back."

Away from the safety of the lamplight, from their quilted beds and hanging bones, they ran toward the woods. The shadows swallowed them up. Hyacinth could feel her heart, hummingbird fast in her chest, could feel the space where fear should have bloomed, filled with something else instead. It was more than hope; it was unchained freedom. It rushed through her blood like wine, and she was dying of thirst.

A laugh bubbled up from her throat, loud and raw, one she had not loosed from her lips before. Beside her, Abelia threw back her head and also laughed. The trees soaked up the sound, adding it to the chorus of savagery as though it had always belonged there. That they belonged there.

The earth beneath their feet muffled the sound of their steps as the roots of the watchful giants burst from the soil, stretching out across the ground. The howling of wildlings fell silent, and Hyacinth's laughter caught in her throat. A heaviness followed the descending quiet. They were being watched. Hyacinth could feel it. Deeper they walked, hands held tight, fingernails digging into palms.

Figures of woven willow branches dangled from above, knotted with bones. They swayed in the subtle breeze, clicking together in a mimicry of the cracking teeth of those who dwelled deeper. Old blood lay stamped across the tree trunks in handprints. Hyacinth stepped closer, splaying out her palm to hover over an imprint. It was larger than hers, the fingers longer. She could not recall whose blood had painted it. Whose bones dangled from above.

Pulling her hand from Abelia's, Hyacinth stretched her arms out wide, tipped her back, and screamed into the woods. It was a call she had heard before, one that echoed across the boughs. She knew it well and sang it as though it belonged to her. It had to; it was hers, and she had claimed it as they would claim her. They had to.

"Sing, Abelia!"

But Abelia remained silent, walking further into the darkness.

"Abelia!" Hyacinth called out, and then she felt it against her chest, in her lungs.

Fear.

"Abelia!"

It crept up her spine like ivy, choking out the wickedness. She took a step backward, another and another, brambles scraping over her face. The bones above her clicked, clicked, clicked. Tapping together like teeth. The trees clicked; the shadows, too. In the darkness, something shifted. The ground trembled, and the bones above her stilled, the clicks now slipping from hungry mouths.

"Abelia, come back!" Hyacinth screamed to the darkness, to the absence.

She spun at the sound of footsteps, hope in her heart. The woods had not spat Abelia out.

"You foolish child!" Her father gripped her wrists, his rough fingers digging in hard. He shook her, rattling her teeth. "Let the oaks have mercy on you, girl, for I will not."

"Abelia is out there." Hyacinth fought to drag her father into the shadows, terror making her bones heavy.

Her father turned, his eyes glowing in a streak of moonlight. "Then pray they have been sated."

Keeping one hand clasped tightly on Hyacinth's arm, he pulled a handful of small bones from the satchel that hung at his hip. They were still wet, sinew and fur dripping onto the soft soil below. With steady breaths, he scattered the remains in a small circle around them while pulling Hyacinth tight to his chest. With the bone circle complete, her father unfolded the mask tied to his belt, the fur, and skin beneath as smooth as leather. He pulled it over his head, and two long ears stood tall, pinned in place with oak twigs. The mouth hole was left bloody, its teeth cracked and yellow.

"Utter not a word, child."

Protests lay heavy on her tongue, but she did as bid and remained silent. She allowed her fear to gag her, allowed it to smother the wickedness she had, for a moment, been high on.

"Close your eyes," her father whispered.

She complied, once again, obedient. Her head pressed against the steady beat of her father's heart. His arms were tight around her, his fingers in her hair, his chin resting on the top of her head. She kept her eyes closed, shutting out the sounds of clicking, of old bone scraping over old bone. Something brushed against her neck, an exhale of breath, heat, and decay. One breath, four breaths... eight...twelve.

The beat of her father's heart slowed, stuttering, his chest no longer moving. Hyacinth took a long, silent inhale and kept it until her lungs burned.

A low, unearthly rattle sounded above her head, an ancient sound, one the trees echoed. Screams answered, the call of the wicked and the wanton and the wild. Tears streamed down Hyacinth's cheeks, a sob wedged in her throat, solid and aching. A mockery of the wicked, sinful screams that had spilled out of her before.

The woods would not eat her that night, but they would not take her either.

With a rigid slowness, her father untangled himself from her, keeping the mask on his face. Hyacinth opened her eyes to see the circle of bones around them remained untouched, but the earth around it lay hewn open. It was a wound scraped raw by stories, legends, the prayers they uttered under candlelight. The Teeth had not eaten her.

They had devoured Abelia.

CHAPTER FOUR

The woods watched them leave. Hyacinth felt it. They let them leave untouched and fearful.

With those watching eyes still watching, they walked back to the village, following the path Hyacinth had danced down with her head tipped back and throat full of song. Shame would soon curdle in her like spoiled milk. But for now, she felt nothing but horror, cooling her blood until she could feel nothing else. Could think of nothing else.

Her tears had left sticky trails over her cheeks, through the dirt caked upon her skin. Hyacinth could smell the woods on her, the blood, the wet bones. The moon shone high above them, the sky clear and full of stars. Often, Hyacinth would lie back in the grass, hands clasped with Abelia's, staring up at the vast expanse of blackness. It was endless, free of the woods around them. She felt a sob threaten to rise.

Abelia, her Abelia, was gone.

Her father's grip bruised her wrist, his cracked fingernails digging into her tender flesh. He smelled of the woods, of moss, and the rot of old bark. Dirt crusted inlay against the lines of his skin, peppering his face. He caught her eye, mouth tight and set.

"Loretta Farley received a public beating for chasing her kitten too close to the woods," he said, his voice gravel rough. He stopped at the edge of the woods, the village just in sight. "Bertie Kewridge took twelve lashings for stealing unblessed twigs. What should we do with you, Hyacinth?"

She looked to the village as a new terror seized her, clinging to her skin like sweat. They had hanged women for less.

The chill of the woods seeped through the fabric of her night-gown. The threat of the noose, of being dragged by the hair through the village, filled her with dread. They could hang her or decide to send her to the Farm, arms thrust out wide, splinters in her mouth. Food for the crows and not the Teeth

"I would rather walk back into the woods," she replied, voice hoarse and trembling. "I would follow Abelia without looking back if it meant denying old men the satisfaction of seeing my swaying body."

Her father sighed, breath shuddering past his lips. He was a tall man, broad-shouldered, with black hair littered with silver at his temples and in his beard. He was a Woodsman, strong and devout, spending his days clearing the path, feeding the trees, stringing up the bones.

But he was afraid.

"I do wish it was not like this, Hyacinth. Do you understand that, at least?"

She shrugged, for what did it matter? Their wishes were as good as their prayers. They all tasted the same. "Then change it."

"Change what? I keep them away, keep them fed, and keep the paths clear so that one day you can go and get away from here."

"To another village…"

"Where you might find happiness."

"With a husband I did not choose."

"It is how it always has been." The wind picked up, rustling the bones at the edge of the woods. "It is what we do to stay safe."

"It's shit."

He barked a laugh. "Of course it is. Do you think you are the only one who wishes for something else, Hyacinth? That no one else wishes their hands weren't stained red?"

"The Elders seem happy."

"There will always be those who accept and crave violence." He let loose his angry grip and pulled her close. "I can't make this world what it is not meant to be, but I can accept my place within it and do what I can to make it safer for you and your sisters. I can't do more than that, Hyacinth. I can't."

She softened in his embrace, enveloping herself in woodsmoke and old blood. There was a strange comfort to it, a weightlessness of being saved. It settled in her stomach, tangling with the longing that remained...and the slow creeping grief growing inside her. Each emotion battled inside her, knotting together until she felt sick.

"Will you speak of what happened tonight?" she asked, keeping her head over the gentle thump of her father's heart. "Beat the wickedness out of me?"

"Not this time, Hyacinth."

"I thought they would take me." She whispered the confession. "I am not good enough for what you and Mother wish for me. But I am not bad enough to slip into the shadows." She pulled back slightly, tilting to meet his eyes. "Where do I fit?"

"What do you want me to tell you?"

"Where do I go?"

"We go home, Hyacinth." He took her hand. "For now, we go home and thank the Oaks that your bones will not be found in the morning. Tomorrow, we will join the others in grieving for the girl who the shadows swallowed up."

For Abelia.

Hyacinth would not have to wait for grief to wrap around her heart, for every memory of her to cut into it. Grief was a wound she would always bear, guilt a knife that would scrape it raw.

CHAPTER FIVE

T he sun rose to the sound of screams. Hyacinth remained in bed, blankets pulled high. Her father had scrubbed the dirt from her face and pulled brambles from her hair. He had been quick and thorough, making no comment on the silent tears tracking down her cheeks.

She had not slept but lay awake staring at the beams overhead. Thick cobwebs clustered the corners, warm and safe beneath the thatch. She watched the spiders weave, unbothered by the world outside their silken threads. As she watched them, Briony watched her, her eyes bright in the darkness. When the screams came, it was Briony who slipped to the side of her bed, her lips close. "I know what you did."

Hyacinth turned away. "I don't know what you're talking about."

"I saw you go into the woods with that Merrow girl. I saw Father drag you back and leave her behind."

"You saw nothing," Hyacinth hissed.

"They will hang you."

"Still your damned tongue!" Celandine tossed the covers off her bed and snatched at Briony's shoulders, shaking her with quick, rough hands. "They will hang the lot of us!"

They both stood in their nightdresses, white and flowing, the same as Hyacinth's. All sewn by their mother's hands, shapeless and modest, like frilled sacks. The morning chill seeped through the gaps in the wood, the bent pieces of the house where the outside drifted in.

"You had nothing to do with any of it," Hyacinth said, voice low.

"You led a girl into the dark," Briony hissed as she wiggled free of Celandine's grasp, "and only you came back. They will burn you as a witch, and the rest of us will dangle, too. They will cut the rot out."

"No one saw..."

"I saw."

The slap echoed, sharp and quick, stinging Hyacinth's palm. "Shut your mouth!"

"Hyacinth!"

Celandine caught her wrist as she made to strike her sister again.

Briony stood gaping, her hand at her cheek. "She hit me!"

"Shut up, Briony." Celandine lowered her voice, glancing over to the small bed where their youngest sibling still slept. Little Elestren did not stir, wrapped tight and safe in her bundle, oblivious to the horrors close by. Hyacinth could not determine if it were a blessing not to know, to linger in those few short years where a mother's arms could shield you from all bad things.

"What happened last night?" Celandine asked. If there was any judgment in her words, Hyacinth could not hear it.

"They were meant to take me." Hyacinth's voice cracked. She rooted for the anger to feel anything except the absence of Abelia. "Father found me instead... I heard them. They were everywhere, above us, near us, and they were famished."

"Oaks save us." The prayer slipped near silent from Briony.

Hyacinth didn't mock her for it, nor did she repeat it. She allowed the words instead to settle upon her to see if they would bring any comfort.

"Wipe the damned guilt from your face," Celandine ordered.

But Hyacinth didn't know how. The guilt had settled into her skin and bled into the wickedness there.

"We were all asleep," Celandine continued. "No one left the cottage, understand? Do you understand, Briony?"

"Yes, stop shaking me."

"We need to get dressed, wake Elestren, and go down together."

Hyacinth returned to her bed and pulled her blankets over her pillow, smoothing out the creases. She straightened the bones at the bedpost, hearing clacking as her sisters did the same. Then she removed her nightgown to put on her green wool dress. It was soft and warm, smelling of home. Homesickness ebbed into the fissures of her heart, and she did not know how best to dig it out.

"I wish you had not come back," Briony hissed, a slowly waking Elestren pressed tight to her chest.

Hyacinth swallowed, turning to Briony so their noses touched. "So do I."

Sunlight bled over the draught-crisp grass, the early morning shadows long and dark. Watery dawn trickled over the treetops, and the wind was quiet. The screams had faded too, slipping into the strange low keening the village knew too well.

The Turning sisters gathered by the bare tables left out from Hyacinth's nameday celebration. The food and drink had long been cleared away, leaving only the antlered skulls on the tabletops, the wildflowers in their eye sockets limp and withered. The bunting hung above them still, little pieces of Hyacinth flapping in the wind. If she had been more devout, she might have seen it as an omen.

They stood in silence with their parents, dressed in their Sermon clothes, silent and waiting. The other families stepped from their houses, too, dressed and washed and brushed respect- fully. Without a word, they reached out their hands, clasping the fingers of their neighbors until there was just one single silent circle. They had done it many times before, stepping out into the morning with a prayer on their lips, reaching out. Waiting. Who knew which sinner would stand in the center, which neighbor, which friend? The Elders knew. Loud women, rueful men. They never came for the quiet ones.

Emory Merrow knelt alone in the center, her nightgown stained with damp earth. She had stopped her awful wailing, the sound now coming from her throat hoarse. One hand stretched out before her toward the woods, fingernails deep in the earth. The other pressed against her heaving chest as though she struggled to keep the pieces of herself together. Not a soul stepped forward to comfort her, though Hyacinth's bones longed to move closer, to curl her hand around the only thing remaining of Abelia.

"The woods were fed here last night!" The booming voice of Elder Thorn shattered the quiet. He stood tall, arms outstretched, looking down on Emory Merrow with a strange light in his eye. Most of his face lay hidden behind his mask, the hollowed hare skin tied neatly with silk ribbon. Its fur was still soft and sleek, unlike the worn, ragged remains of her father's mask. The ears stood up straight, pinned with silver and not wood. Even the teeth were polished white.

Elder Thorn was hungry, too. Not for blood and bone, not like the Teeth. But for the fear they carried, for a mother's grief, for the power that followed it. Hyacinth saw it.

"Abelia Merrow stole from her bed in the night and went into the darkness. She heard the calling of the wild ones, and it called to her, to her wicked soul." Elder Thorn stepped into the circle, kneeling beside Emory, robes of ruddy brown splaying out around him. The color of old, dried blood. "Did she not say her prayers?"

"Every night, Elder Thorn." Emory breathed, head bent low.

"Wear her Oak?"

Emory clutched harder at her chest, her fingers reaching for the wooden circlet at her neck. "She never took it off."

"Did you birth a witch, Mrs. Merrow?"

They were all witches, the wicked women, the women who looked beyond the lantern glow of the doorways, beyond the dangling bones.

Witches because someone said so.

"She was a good girl," Emory's voice cracked, tears choking her. "A good girl, I swear to you."

"Good girls don't go wandering into the woods." Elder Lachlan stepped into the circle. He was a thin man with thinner hair, his smile a little too crooked. He wore the mask of a winter hare, the fur a perfect, innocent white. "We can't have children thinking they can just slip into the shadows, Mrs. Merrow, can we? The trees will grow greedy, and we will no longer be safe."

A collective gasp shuddered through the circle, the villagers taking a step back as one, their arms still stretched, still clutching the fingers of their neighbors. Hyacinth kept her eyes on Emory, wishing she could kneel beside her and share in her grief and loss. Celandine tightened her grip on Hyacinth's hand, her fingernails pinching hard, leaving welts. Her sister silently spoke what Hyacinth knew: she couldn't move, couldn't own up to her wickedness.

"Who tended the eastern path last night?" Elder Lachlan called out, his spine straightened with self-importance.

"I was there."

The circle jolted as her father entered it. Although he was much taller and broader than Elder Lachlan, it was clear who held the power.

Elder Lachlan's eyes burned as he stared at her father, placing a weathered hand upon Emory's shoulder. "And what did you see?"

Hyacinth stared at her father's back, willing her nerves to calm so that her face would not betray all she was trying to hide. She could prevent the secrets from spilling out—bite through her tongue if she had to—but keeping the truth out of her eyes or the color of her skin as dread leached it away would prove difficult. She was a map of sins if anyone looked close enough to read her.

"They found something," her father said. "I believe they ate something last night."

Emory slipped forward, a ragged sound tearing from her throat.

Hyacinth watched, unmoving, as her father slipped down beside Emory, his voice carrying across the grass.

"I will go back and find what I can."

"You will leave her heathen bones where they lie!" Elder Thorn grabbed Emory by the arm, hauling her to her feet. "If it is the woods she chose, then let them keep her soul."

"I beg mercy of you, please..."

"I have the mercy of all to consider, Mrs. Merrow." He forced her up. "The mother of a witch is a witch in the eyes of the woods."

Shouts rose. People who had once bought Emory Merrow's blackberry jam and worn the knitted shawls she spent summers making were now calling for her death with cruel enthusiasm.

They were afraid. Hyacinth knew that. Afraid and bored and awful. They were all awful, the Elders most of all.

For a moment, Emory stood quite still, her kind face twisted by something unreadable. She locked eyes with Hyacinth, and Hyacinth saw. She knew. Keeping her dark eyes fixed on Hyacinth, Emory Merrow sucked in a breath and spat thickly onto Elder Lachlan's masked cheek, staining that awful white.

Then she tore away from his grasp and, with a shrieking sob, darted to the trees to the clean-picked bones of her daughter.

Hyacinth wanted to scream after her, to urge her to run faster, to find the parts of Abelia left behind so she could put them beneath the earth. But she could do nothing but watch as Emory made it to the creeping shadow and stopped. She arched back, soundless, and fell, one roughly carved arrow protruding from her eye.

CHAPTER SIX

They burnt Emory Merrow at nightfall.

The thick smoke gathered quickly, rising up to darken the early twilit sky. Flames licked at her body, almost gentle. It was a quick death, merciful, and Hyacinth knew how much it disappointed the Elders. There was little enjoyment in burning a dead woman.

Hyacinth stood at the edge, away from her parents and sisters. She wore her best dress, her tangles tied back with ribbon. The reek of burning flesh filled her nose, the crackling wood sounding all too similar to the clicking of teeth. The flames would take Emory's soul, and her blackened bones would be used to keep the village safe. The heat seeped into Hyacinth's own bones, taking the chill of the night away. She almost stepped closer to warm herself on someone's funeral pyre.

The Elders stood in the inner circle with their masks and robes and thirst for sins. Twelve of them, with words powerful enough to set flesh on fire, to break necks, to force splinters onto the tongues of those deemed unworthy. Hyacinth wondered what she would do with such power if granted to her. Would she be better or just as hungry?

Most of them were bent over with age, all thinning hair and plump bellies, but there were a few much younger, nearer her age, granted safety and privilege only a fool would turn down. Elder Sparrow looked foolish enough, his robes too long, his mask seemingly always askew no matter how much he tied the ribbons. It had been a task, sitting so close to Abelia while he stumbled over his sermons, biting back the laughter that would send them both to a whipping.

A fool of a man. It would have been better to feed him to the Teeth, Hyacinth often thought. Let him be useful, if only for a moment.

Beside him, only a few summers older than Hyacinth, stood Elder Reed. His robes fitted him better, and his mask was tight and freshly skinned. He was no young fool. There had been no sounds of stifled laughter when he stood and spoke. She would always look closely at his hands, wishing to know how he was able to scrub the blood and sins off them. Wondering why his sins seemed to matter less, why heads were turned, eyes diverted to reap the wrongs of others.

No, if Hyacinth were granted the life of an Elder, she was certain she would not be good at all.

Looking across the smoke, she caught Elder Lachlan's eye. He did not watch Emory burn but instead kept his gaze on Hyacinth. She stared back, wondering which parts of her he saw. The soft wool dress and good stockings, the ribbon in her hair...or was he looking deeper, thirsting to find a reason to char the skin from her bones?

With a lift of his lips, Elder Lachlan turned away. He walked close enough to the pyre that black dust gathered on the downy white of his mask. Hyacinth braced herself for the words he would hiss at her, the warnings. But he did not step up to her, but her father. With a touch of his shoulder and a nod, he beckoned her father to follow.

Dread coiled low in Hyacinth's belly, threading around the knotted grief until she feared she would vomit it all up and everyone would see the sins she had choked down. She watched her father go, and so did her mother, wide-eyed and pale. Her sisters watched, too. Elestren cried out, her little arms reaching. Briony staggered backward, past Hyacinth, her hand tight to her mouth.

"What did you do?" Hyacinth chased after her, her words quiet, vicious.

Her sister heaved into the grass, bringing up porridge and not sins. "They said..."

"What have you done?" The words had teeth, and how she wished she could use them. "Briony!"

"I did as you asked—I kept quiet! I did, I really did." She fell to the ground, looking up at Hyacinth with terrified eyes and shaking hands. "The Elders asked if I had seen anything, and I said no. I said no, Hyacinth, I promise!"

"I don't believe you."

"They asked me when Father came home if I heard him come home..."

"And what did you tell them?"

"That I heard the door late in the night, no later than he usually comes in." Briony paused, lips trembling. She bit her lower lip until blood collected at the corners of her mouth. "I said...I said I heard the door lock, and I fell asleep as he said goodnight."

"Goodnight to whom?" Hyacinth hissed, knowing.

"I never said your name."

"I could have just been waiting up for him! Rosealie Heath does so for her father every night when she's not rutting that Barrow boy in the stables."

"They found the bone circle."

"All the Woodsmen leave bone circles."

"Big enough for two?" Briony wiped her mouth, taking a long, shuddering breath. "You did this, Hyacinth. Blame no one else but yourself."

Evening had slipped over the house before her father came home. They sat around their table, still as the glow from their waning candles. Hyacinth sat closest to the window, watching the neighbors light their porch lanterns. Watching the Woodsmen as they wandered out into the dark, masks at their hips, bags of bones at hand. Her father did not walk among them.

Her mother had paced the floors until late afternoon, brushing away the cups of over-brewed tea Briony offered her. She ignored Celandine's firm words and barked at her to calm herself and sit down. She held onto Elestren, tiny and innocent and blameless, keeping her at her hip.

She would not look at Hyacinth.

At the sound of the door creaking open, they all stood. Hyacinth stepped forward, pushing closer, needing to dampen the knot in her stomach before it pulled her down into the ground beneath. Her father stood in the doorway, his shoulders sloping as if burdened by unseen weight.

"Am I to hang?" Hyacinth kept her chin up, wondering if she would make it to the Shadows before they shot her down. If she would make it further than Emory Merrow.

"Oaks bless us," murmured her mother. Elestren let out a shrill cry, no doubt from being squeezed too firmly. "We will all hang."

"Not if we cast her out!" Briony pointed a finger, and Hyacinth sneered at it.

"Your piousness may save you yet."

"And your heathen ways have damned you!"

"Fuck off."

"Hyacinth!" With one free hand, her mother struck her, stinging Hyacinth's cheek. Then she gripped her shoulder, fingers tight on her good wool dress. "Hold your tongue."

"No one gets a hanging from swearing, Mother," Celandine pointed out, remaining, like their father, stoic and calm. "If they did, Hyacinth would be long gone."

"What did they say, Rowan?" Their mother pushed past them to claw at the shirtsleeves of her husband. "Has she damned us all?"

"She ain't hanging. Not this time."

"Praise their mercy!" Still clinging to Elestren, their mother fell to her knees, tears slipping down her cheeks.

"What price did you pay for my neck, Father?" Hyacinth asked, not joining her mother in her weeping or her sister's silent relief. Her cheek throbbed, the taste of blood warm on her tongue. "What are we to give to the Elders for the benevolence they would not impart on a grieving mother?"

"Your hand."

"To whom?"

"You are to wed Elder Reed this coming summer, Hyacinth. You will do it with a smile, without your wicked tongue and wicked ways and want of the woods...."

"No—"

"Then we all hang." Her father gripped her arms, shaking her firmly. There were always people shaking her. "Your mother and your sisters, too. Even Little Elestren. They will find rope for them all and scatter your bones to the woods."

Hyacinth stood rigid. "You would give me away to such a man as Elder Reed? You have heard the stories, the awful things he has done? He is a monster, Father."

She had hoped to stoke sympathy in her father, for her words to soften the look on his face, the grip on her arms. He held her tighter instead, fingertips pressing hard enough to bruise.

"I will not be giving you away, Hyacinth."

She realized then, with a cold, sickening dread, that the full price of her salvation laid bare. She caught it before the others, felt it in the way her father held her. The bruises his fingers made would fade, but she wanted them etched into her skin.

"Rowan?" Her mother's voice slipped quietly, a thread of hope lingering on his name. A fragile thing, a gossamer hope.

"You will all be safe," her father said, unwavering, rough and calm and strong. He did not let Hyacinth go. "You will receive a widow's wage, Brona. The girls will marry, and you will be safe."

He did not look to Hyacinth, did not share that promise with her. She would not get the rope; therefore, she should be thankful.

"They will hang you in Hyacinth's stead," Celandine said, no question on her lips.

Their father nodded. "Quietly, just the Elders and the hanging tree."

Hyacinth's mother let out a horrible cry, hands still clutching Elestren tight. It was a different cry than Emory Merrow's, as though the child clasped to her breast had muffled it.

Briony sank beside her, her good dress wrinkling over the floor-boards. Celandine remained standing, her wide eyes fixed on their father. She would not look at Hyacinth—no one would look at her. Hyacinth found herself yearning for just one kind word, a soft nod of the head, a deliverance from the guilt and shame and grief that battered her insides. But she dared not reach out to seek the comfort she craved. The lack of it was unbearable, but a rejection would shatter her.

CHAPTER SEVEN

T he Hanging Tree stood away from the woods, down from
the village, along a twisting pathway kept clear by the
Woodsmen. It was an ancient oak, sacred like the saplings
they made their carvings from to hang around their necks. It was
bent, moss-covered, and creaking, a waiting executioner. Around it,
a circle of bones, yellowed with age, belonging to those who had
swung from its branches. A sinner's fence. Dead grass lay beneath,
rustling in the evening breeze.

Hyacinth and her family walked down together, following the
winding pathway they had all walked before, the stones beneath
their feet worn smooth. Hyacinth kept her footsteps slow, lingering
a little behind the procession as if it would buy her father time. If
perhaps she looked good, innocent, and sorry, then the Elders
would not make posts from his bones. A reprieve, though rare, was
not unheard of. Her father was a good man, a good Woodsman.
Perhaps this was to be his only punishment, the walk, the feel of his
death in the air. Perhaps he would be allowed to go home, shaken
and weary but repentant. Hyacinth would be good; she would echo
the sermons, she would hold her Oak, she would say her prayers,
and she would fight to believe the words.

Her mother's loud sobs had quieted lest the neighbors come to see where the Turning family headed. She kept her head bowed with Elestren at her hip, her hands gripping the blanket her daughter was wrapped in.

Briony held their mother up, her head high, silent tears down her pious face. She had straightened her dress, brushed out her tangles, and wiped any residue of Hyacinth's wickedness from her skin. She had turned, only once, to spit at Hyacinth's feet.

"That rope should be yours," she had hissed. "Yours alone."

"They are not hanging father as a witch," Hyacinth said in return, the words low enough that their mother did not hear. "If it were a rope for my neck, you would be swinging right alongside me."

With a slow, awful smile, Briony slipped away from their mother's grip, coming close enough to touch noses with Hyacinth. She smelled the mint tea on her breath, sharp and bitter, and the swirls of gold in her dark eyes. "I hope Elder Reeds pulls you through those trees screaming. I hope he makes a good wife of you."

Hyacinth drew close, her teeth almost grazing Briony's plump cheek. Her sister flinched as though fearing the sharpness of Hyacinth's words.

"I will make him scream. I promise you that," she hissed.

"You heathen whore."

"Such a tongue on you, sister dear. Careful, or someone might just cut it from your mouth."

Hyacinth brushed past her sister and her mother to fall into step with her father. Celandine caught her eye. There was a coldness there, an accusation she did not voice but that Hyacinth could hear as though she screamed it. She wished she would scream it. To hear from Celandine meant something, something Briony's words could never mean.

"I have asked your sister to watch over the others." Her father nodded to Celandine, who slowed her steps, falling behind with their mother and Briony. No tremor shook his flint-sharp voice. "What can I ask of you, Hyacinth?"

"Anything."

"Would you lie to a dying man?"

"Father..."

He bowed, the scruff on his chin scratching against her face. "There may be something beyond the woods."

Hyacinth pulled back, her reply laced with hope. "Better?"

"I know not." His words scratched against her wickedness, raking it raw. "Look toward the clearing, Hyacinth. Away from the Teeth."

"Would you send me through the woods?" she whispered, the blasphemy sweet on her tongue. "They hungered for my bones."

"You will have to choose the teeth that feast upon you." Her father turned his head, eyes fixing upon the small group of Elders waiting to snap his neck. "I can offer you no more than that. Forgive me, Hyacinth."

"For what?" Her fingers dug into her father's shirt, scratching the skin beneath. Soon, they would pry them apart, but for a moment, she pretended her hold on her father was enough.

"I cannot save you, Hyacinth," he said, his gentle blue eyes lined with tears. "But by the Oaks, I did try."

The Elders stood ahead, dressed in robes with their carrion masks and carved bones at their hips. Although Hyacinth could not see their faces, she knew they smiled. Behind the smooth hare skin, they were gleeful. They had missed out on burning Emory Merrow, had been denied her screams and her bones and her soul. They would take her father to sate their hunger, blameless as he was. Not the endless appetites of the Teeth, but of men.

Her father uncurled the fingers that held him, bringing them briefly to his lips before letting her hand drop. They would never hold her again.

One by one, he embraced his family, bringing little Elestren close as though committing her scent to memory. She babbled at him with bubbles on her lips, not understanding they wouldn't be bringing him back home.

Hyacinth wished she shared her youngest sibling's naivety.

Lastly, he embraced their mother. Drawing her to him, and as she wept in his arms, he cracked, his knees buckling so they slipped to the ground together. They came to rip him away from her, and he went without protest. Hyacinth wanted him to run, to make for the Shadows, to the Teeth beyond, because he knew the woods well. He knew every tree, and if anyone could slip beneath them and remain whole, Hyacinth knew it would be him.

"Run," she said through gritted teeth. "Run, run, run, run..."

A hand gripped her wrist, pulling sharply so her knees thudded to the ground. Her mother loosened her hold, and her hand slipped into Hyacinth's. "Do not watch, child."

But watch, she did.

With a cruel, deliberate slowness, they led him to the stool, slipping the worn noose around his neck. They took away her father's life in silence, allowing him no words of comfort, mercy, or salvation. The stool rocked, wood creaking, tilting. The drop wasn't enough to break his neck, but it left him dangling. The rope groaned, threads splitting with the weight of her father. His legs kicked, bucked, fought. His face reddened, the skin mottling to an awful purple, his dark eyes wide, frightened, and desperate. And then he stilled.

The Elders left him in silence, leaving him to sway in the breeze like the bones tied to the branches beyond.

Hyacinth watched on, one hand in her mother's, the other clawing at the earth, her fingernails cracking on flint.

Blood trickled from her nail beds, and she forced her hand deeper so the soil would soak it up. She hoped the woods could taste it, her fear dribbling out until nothing but her wickedness remained. She kept watching, her gaze unrelenting on the silent Elders, even as they began to disperse.

"I will feed them to the Teeth," she whispered. She turned to her mother. "And leave their bones for the crows."

Her mother said nothing, but with a slow, knowing bob of her head, she nodded.

CHAPTER EIGHT

The leaves had shifted to brown by Hyacinth's wedding day. The Elders would not wait until the following summer, with the scent of wildflowers on the breeze and the grass crisp beneath her bare feet. She was to be wed in haste and sent away.

The breeze carried with it the rumor of an early frost and a cruel winter to follow. It snatched at Hyacinth's hair, tearing it free from the braid Briony's cold fingers had forced it into. Few flowers were left on the ground, just the late-blooming idleweed, a white-headed flower that grew in the shadows close to the trees. They were thought to be unlucky, a bad omen.

Hyacinth threaded them through her wild strands anyway, knotting them into a crown in place of a veil. At her hip, she wore the soft silk purse her mother had made for her, similar to the ones her elder sisters wore on their wedding days. Lace trimmed the edge, needlessly expensive. Inside were the bones she had gathered, the hind of a hare, ribs of a shrew, the delicate long-beaked skull of a kingfisher. Hyacinth had skinned them herself, sitting at the kitchen table with her mother's knife, slewing off flesh and feather in silence. Her mother hovered, her lips firm in a tight line, holding back criticism and judgment as she watched. Hyacinth felt them anyway, the unspoken words, the way they pressed heavy in the air with everything else unsaid.

"You look beautiful."

Her mother's words pushed through, falling with a strange hollowness on Hyacinth's ears. It was easy to be beautiful, washed, and dressed up like a doll, all sins and wickedness hidden beneath layers of white and the scent of lavender.

Her mother fussed with the lace of Hyacinth's dress and the silk ribbons at her waist, all paid for by her generous bridegroom. She said nothing of the rumors, of the cruel hands and sharp tongue he offered. Any sorrow her mother felt remained hidden by a well-practiced smile. Everyone wore their own masks, and Hyacinth wanted to burst with the screams she held behind hers.

"You make a lovely sacrifice," Celandine said, dragging a comb through Elestren's ebony curls. "A perfect little lamb."

It was the closest she would get to what they were all thinking, and it wasn't enough.

Hyacinth curtsied. "Will you miss me?"

A tear escaped Celandine's eye and dashed away before anyone, but Hyacinth could see. "Like you are taking a piece of me away with you."

Hyacinth did not ask Briony. There lay a chasm between them, gorged wider as summer spilled into autumn. It was full of unspoken, spiteful words and hateful silence. The tentative sisterly bond they once shared was long gone.

She missed it sometimes, late at night when she heard the soft, rumbling snores of slumber. A grieving of something irreparably lost, a memory of a time before, of something no longer hers.

It was a feeling she did not care for.

"Will you miss me, Mother?" The question fell softly, and Hyacinth almost wished she had not voiced it, afraid of the answer. She could not bear to leave without a kind word to keep her company. She and her mother never shared a closeness, each reaching out at different moments, brushing past without quite touching.

"I feel the absence of all my children," her mother replied. "Your sisters have long since gone, wedded well and content. I feel the loss of them eat at my heart and claw at it in moments of silence, the pain often so I can scarcely breathe."

A firm hand cupped Hyacinth's chin, forcing her gaze. Grief had darkened her mother's eyes, but they were sharp as they bore deep into Hyacinth's. "Your parting, girl, will consume whatever is left, leaving nothing for those you leave behind."

Hyacinth allowed her mother to fuss over her one last time as though they could force years of distance and misunderstanding closer in the span of a few heartbeats. Cool fingers brushed over the loose strands of her hair, her nose, and her lips, imparting her features to memory. She slipped a copper coin into the purse at Hyacinth's hip, a token for a rich life. It rattled the bones: the hare, the shrew, and the bird, and unknown to her mother, the single white finger bone she had picked from the Sinner's fence.

The entire village gathered to watch Hyacinth exchange her vows, all seated upon mismatched chairs and stools. A feast awaited them, a spitted hog cooked long and slow over flame. It filled the air with the stench of greasy fat, a reminder of what she would have smelled like if not for the Elder's mercy.

They hanged cowards and traitors, thieves and miscreants. They seldom hanged their witches.

Hyacinth stepped down the narrow aisle alone, holding her chin high, caring little for the scorn and pity tossed her way. There were whispers as she passed; some clutched the Oaks around their necks tighter, and someone spat at her feet. A coward's daughter sent away in shame.

It was unforgivable for a Woodsman to fail to keep the village safe.

Hyacinth stopped at the altar, the smooth wood covered with frayed white cloth and the freshly skinned bones of a hare. A brass cup of blood glistened beneath the high sun. She could smell the copper tang, already feel its warmth against her throat.

She was thankful she had refused breakfast.

Elder Reed stood beside her with his mask off, carved bones clenched in his fist. His hair was the color of old wheat and had been combed back from his eyes. He would have been handsome, and perhaps he was, but his eyes were cold, the line of his jaw tense. Hyacinth would have much preferred Angus Bartleby.

He did not smile when she stepped up beside him, but his eyes strayed to the luckless flowers in her hair, his lip curling. She realized she didn't even know his name. Was she to refer to him as Elder Reed? Perhaps as Sir, with her head bowed. If that were what was expected of her, then she would remain silent. She would rather swallow her own tongue.

"Our blessed day!" Elder Lachlan declared from his place behind the altar. The sunlight gleamed off the fresh blood at his fingertips. "We stand joined at the end of a long and hot summer, one that has been tainted with the cries of the heathens..."

"Bless us!" the villagers cried a soulful echo.

Hyacinth said nothing at all.

Elder Reed's lips thinned even more until she feared they would split apart from his face.

Elder Lachlan outstretched his hands, performing to his crowd of devout followers. "We gather here to join the hands of our fellow Elder to Hyacinth Turning, daughter of a coward, as is our mercy."

Hyacinth's smile slipped, and she gripped the purse at her hip tight, feeling for the bones inside. It was the story given to the village that Rowan Turning had failed in his duties to protect a child from the woods. The families of cowards were looked after if they paid penance, and by the trees, they had done so.

Hyacinth was the last payment to be given.

She looked to Elder Reed, her future husband, not needing him to speak to know he would not be kind to her. The others wanted him gone from the village, struggling to hide rumor after rumor of his depravity. She was as much his punishment as he was to her.

"We taste the blood to taste our sins."

The cup was lifted to Hyacinth's lips and poured slowly so the thickness coated her mouth. She swallowed, eyes firm on Elder Lachlan as she slid her tongue over her teeth.

She kept his gaze while he offered the cup to Elder Reed and wondered if blood still stained her lips. She turned as her betrothed drank, a heavy gulp against the quiet. He quickly dabbed the dribble of red on his chin.

"We cross our hands with blood to remind us to sate the hunger," Elder Lachlan continued, gesturing for Hyacinth and Elder Reed to lift their palms.

Hyacinth swept hers forward, unflinching as her bridegroom closed his long fingers over hers. The rest of the hare blood was poured over their hands, their wrists, until it ran down their arms to pool at her feet.

It splattered on the perfect white of her gown.

The skinned bones were next, carved and waiting. A handful was given to her first to place with care in the silk pouch. They rattled against the others, the fresh blood soaking through the silk in a slowly growing stain.

"Carve the bones. One for the gate, one for the door, two for the mantel, and three for the floor."

"Carve the bones," Hyacinth murmured, quicker than Elder Reed. He fumbled over his words, all three of them. She heard someone behind her snigger. From the familiar sound, she guessed it was Celandine, and her heart ached.

"The path lies clear." Elder Lachlan swept his arm behind him with an exaggerated flounce. "The bones of Mrs. Merrow will guide you through. Let the winds rattle through them and keep the teeth from your flesh. The trees are sated."

"The trees are sated." Hyacinth's mouth moved to the words, but she would not speak them.

Emory Merrow's bones had been hung high up in the branches, higher than most, so they would be nowhere near the picked remains of her daughter. Hyacinth clutched at her silken purse tighter, noting how the blood spread out against the soft white like a bandaged wound.

Emory's bones would see her through the woods, and unbeknown to the Elders, so would the bones of Hyacinth's father.

Hyacinth danced with the boys from the village, with most of the girls, too. She held the hand of her mother, with little Elestren on her hip, and danced to the fading light of the setting sun. It bled over the trees, feeding the shadows until they stretched and gorged over the brittle grass.

Celandine held onto her the longest, her sun-browned hands tight over hers.

Hyacinth gripped her sister back just as tightly as though it mattered.

"I was too young to miss Heather and Dilly," her sister said as she lifted Hyacinth's hand to her lip. She seemed not to mind the brownish tint of Hyacinth's skin. "I was too young to understand that they would go into the woods and not return. But I think even if it were Briony setting out, perhaps even Elestren and I were to be left behind, I would not worry as much as I worry for you."

"Because of the trees?" Hyacinth began, wondering if the bones of Emory Merrow would be enough to stop the Teeth from feasting upon her. "Because I am wicked?"

"You know why."

She turned, bridal gown splattered with blood and dirt, hem yellowed by the grass. She saw her new husband standing afar, clothed in shadow, his mask of fur pulled down over his eyes. She still had not learned his name, had yet to speak to him at all.

He had not asked her to dance, and she had not cared.

"I think we are to be each other's misery," she said, not turning back, ensuring he saw the words on her lips. That she knew.

"You deserved Angus."

A laugh cracked free. "Aye, I did." Hyacinth tore her gaze from her husband to find the boy who had requested her hand. She never asked who any of the others had been. Angus had been enough. "Maybe he'll ask for your hand."

"And if I do not want him?"

There was a trace of humor to her voice, a softness to the edges of it that did not quite fit. The loss of their father had carved away the jagged pieces of Celandine, leaving crevices for the wickedness to seep out and away. It had curved her inward, forced her gaze downward.

"Do not leave him for Briony," Hyacinth said, squeezing her sister's hand tighter. "If he asks for you, you must accept."

"And who will look after Mother?"

"Let Briony. You know she enjoys the self-sacrifice. After that, it will be Elestren, and after her, she will have to fall upon the mercy and kindness of the village."

"And if they will not help her?"

Hyacinth gave a small shrug. "Then she must care for herself."

"Can she?"

Hyacinth took her hand back, running it over the stains in her gown. "We all have to."

The music continued, soft notes slipping over the darkening skies. Fiddles carved from the evergreen spruces played out the songs of the Woods, and hare-gut strings mimicked the sound of the wind. Drums lent a heady thunder, their pale skins drawn tight, reverberating with every beat of smooth, worn bone. From the edges of the village, the Woodsmen returned weary and dirty. The paths leading Hyacinth away had been cleared, the creeping vines stripped back, roots dug up, boughs removed. New bones would have been hung to keep those hungering for her flesh away. But Hyacinth had seen them, heard them. Sometimes, the bones kept them away, and sometimes, they did not.

She walked alone back to the cottage, leaving behind the sound of dancing and merrymaking. The scent of home settled against her, a perfume of tea and smoke and sweat. It was hers, made up of all of them; there would be nothing like it again.

Hyacinth slipped the ruined silk from her shoulders, folding it with unnecessary care onto her bed. It would be torn to pieces, the scraps used to join the other pieces of fabric that had once touched her skin. Hyacinth put on her best wool dress, tucking the carved bones that hung from her bedposts beneath the small bundle of clothing she had packed. Everything was wrapped up in her bed blanket, and she clasped it tight, feeling its warmth and comfort, and the safety it had once offered her.

CHAPTER NINE

T he wood of the carriage was etched so deeply that it had split, the carvings ruddy with old blood. Bones hung from the fixings, clacking together, joining the clacking of bones tied to the lone horse that pulled them along. Her mother and sisters saw her off, their hands sorrow-tight, leaving bruises. They would fade, just as the bruises of her father's frantic hands had faded. There would soon be no marks upon her, nothing to tell her she once belonged to them. And nothing left to remind them of her. Her smell, the imprint she left upon her mattress, would fade, just as her elder sisters' had faded. She would become only a memory, a shared ache.

Elestren would not remember her.

Briony had even held her for a moment, though she said nothing. No words could be spoken between them that could bridge the chasm they had carved between one another.

And then she was sent away, beside a man she had no name for, who was also being sent away for being too awful.

Perhaps they would make a good pairing.

They rode along the path cleared by the Woodsman in silence. "No one told me how long our journey will be." Hyacinth broke it, shifting on the hard wooden seat beside her new husband. "Are we going to camp in the woods?"

Elder Reed kept his masked gaze forward, his hands stiff on the reins. "Are you afraid?"

"Of the trees or of you?"

"You tell me."

She rolled her eyes, stretching out her legs so they rested on the bar in front of her. "Neither."

"If we stop, they may sense your heathen heart, Hyacinth, and step across the path, be it cleared or not."

"I am a fast runner."

"You cannot outrun the Teeth."

She turned to him, catching the darkness beneath the old mask, the pale lashes standing out from the shadows of his face. "I can outrun you, and I think that is all that matters."

"Do you now." His voice was rough, a low scratching from his throat. He had watched her father swing from the Sinner's Tree and smiled.

"Tell me your name, husband mine." Hyacinth noted the pinch of his lips at her demand. She would not ask politely. She had decided long before that she would give no part of herself away—neither her heart nor her body—if he did not let go of this simple thing of his.

"Sorrell."

"Sorrell," she repeated, feeling the way her mouth shaped the word and fell softly from her tongue. It was a whisper of a name, a gentle thing. If there was a time when it had suited him, when he could carry its softness and have it fit as a name should, then he had long outgrown it.

"I would prefer you call me Elder Reed," he snapped.

"Well, I would prefer I were not married to you at all," she snapped back, slipping off her boots to feel the cool air on her feet. "So here we are."

"I will not have such tongue from you, wife."

"And what will you do, husband? What others before you have failed to do?"

"You will fear me, and you will respect me."

"We shall see."

The carriage continued to follow the winding pathway. Hyacinth kept her gaze to the darkness, looking for signs of movement, for the sound of bones clicking, for the Teeth...or the shrill call of the wild women the woods had claimed for their own. She longed to hear the women once more, but for days they had been silent.

But the woods were sated; she could almost hear them sigh, filled with the souls of heathens and cowards. They allowed Hyacinth and her husband to pass, and she had to bite her tongue to stop herself from screaming through the boughs. Anything would be better than what lay ahead.

Once they arrived at the new village, she would be expected to bear children, raise them to be good, and send them along the path to do it all over again. Keep the stories alive, feed the trees, fear the woods, obey the Elders.

Ignore the call of the wild women, the heathens. They do not sing for you.

She had been too sure they had, the way their song had scorched her blood, heated Abelia's, and lured them both with a feral hymn.

Abelia. The grief of her father's passing had overshadowed her memory, but not for too long. She remembered her smile, the way it would make her nose crinkle. She remembered the feel of her hair, the tangles of it, the hues of black, brown, and tawny gold, unbound and caught by the wind. They shared breath and heart-beats, their fingers clasped while they lay on the damp earth, staring upwards. They were closer than sisters ever could be, some-thing Hyacinth had no words for but that she felt. It had thrummed deep within her breast, a warmth she cherished.

And it was gone.

The turn of summer brought evening upon them quickly, and

soon, the meager light from the swaying carriage lantern created dancing shadows around them. Hyacinth continued to focus on the dark shapes in the woods, watching, but nothing stepped out into their path. Nothing moved.

There was no sign of life beneath the boughs, no rustle of footsteps, no cry of owl or fox or deer. It was a preternatural quiet, and it rattled Hyacinth's bones, made her muscles ache with tension. Beside her, Sorrell also sat quietly, looking just as uncomfortable as she.

"I think they are watching us," Hyacinth whispered, leaning closer. He smelled of sweat and old grass. "If you look closely at the shadows, you can see them."

Sorrell's shoulders hunched, a tiny movement, but Hyacinth saw. "Let the Oaks bless us here and allow the sinful bones to keep those with hunger away." His hand reached for the wooden circlet at his neck. "I have carved my bones, and I wear them well. Let the Oaks carry me on."

"Carve the bones," Hyacinth said with a smile. "Have you seen them, husband?"

"Hush your blasphemy..."

"I have seen them," she continued, words low. "Is that why you will not look? Do you not know what hides in those shadows?"

"It is the Woodsmen's lot to set eyes on them; mine is to swallow your sins and save your soul."

"Do you really believe that?"

His silence was answer enough.

The evening darkness grew heavier, and soon, Hyacinth could no longer fight the lull of the swaying carriage. She had never fallen asleep without the slumbering sounds of her sisters nearby nor the soft babbling of Elestren. She dreamed still, as though she were still beneath the eaves of her home, under the blanket woven by her mother's hands, protected by the wood carved by her father.

She soon heard the familiar song, the lullaby of wicked tongues and bare feet, of filthy hems and unwed hands. It echoed throughout her cottage, winding its way up the stairs like a ghost, tendrils of music splaying out, branches tangling through her hair, around her arms to haul her from bed. She followed, her feet cold on the damp ground, nightgown blowing around her ankles, her skin illuminated by the fat moon hanging above.

"Come!" Abelia caught her hand, her fingers cold and firm. The breeze snatched at her hair, disturbing the moss and twigs entangled within. "Come and listen, Hyacinth."

"I can hear it!"

"Come and see!"

Abelia tugged, and Hyacinth followed. They spun, twirling to the chorus rattling through the branches, to the clacking of bones, to the creaking of colossal jaws lost in the darkness.

Fear slithered over her skin, chilling the dirt-sodden sweat, so she halted with a shiver. Abelia danced on. Arms outstretched, standing on pointed toes with flesh split and bleeding. Abelia's exposed bones gleamed in the moonlight, her muscles loose like strings of ivy. She held out a crooked, flesh-stripped hand. "Do not leave me to dance alone."

She cocked her head. Her hair fell in knotted clumps over her shoulder bone, stained by mud and moss. The flesh there stretched as thin as a moth wing, the edges blackened. Hyacinth could see Abelia's ribs tremble with each rasping breath she took.

"Come back with me, Abelia," Hyacinth stammered. She tasted the rot on Abelia's tongue, curdling her stomach, the richness of damp soil sticking in her throat.

"We want your heathen heart," Abelia answered, twirling still, the bone of her ankles creaking, scraping over bloodied earth. With a crack, her foot turned and snapped nearly free. Abelia fell and laughed. "Your wicked soul, your bitter whore mouth."

Frozen in place, Hyacinth could barely rasp out a broken "Stop!"

Blackened ivy and withered root curled over Abelia's twisted foot, lacing sinew and splintered bone together. Hyacinth wanted her to stay down, to not move, to not come closer. She also wanted to stay, to embrace her, to scream and sing and weep.

"Come dance with me, Hyacinth! Come dance with us."

"I am afraid!"

Abelia stepped forward, limping, falling, crawling. Moss spread up over her arms, her legs.

"You were."

Hyacinth jolted awake with a gasp, sucking in air between her teeth. Sorrell was watching her with his thin lip curled, the reins slack in his hands. She stared back, not lifting her head from where it rested against the back of the seat.

"You are quite the restless sleeper," Elder Reed said, disgust in his voice. "Flaying about and muttering to yourself. It is most unbecoming. You are to stop that at once."

She wiped the drool from her chin with the back of her hand. She could still taste the dream, the blood, and the soil, could still hear the echoes of Abelia's call in her mind.

"It is said only witches can control dreaming," she answered, looking up at the dark branches above her. "Do you honestly think me a witch?"

"I guess we shall see."

"But what do you think, Sorrell?" she pressed, noting the way his eyes hardened at his name on her lips. "Did your fellow Elders wed you to a wildling? To a child of the trees? A whore to the Teeth? What must they think of you—"

The slap stole her breath and shoved the words back down her throat. She tasted metallic salt and let the blood dribble over her lips.

"Do not bait me, Hyacinth." He pulled a white handkerchief from his pocket and dabbed them. "You will not like the consequences. Be quiet, be gentle, be good, and I won't have to hurt you."

Her cheek was aflame, yet she resisted the urge to hold it. She narrowed her eyes and gave him a curt nod instead, remaining silent. She swallowed her rage, along with the blood, and let it smolder within.

CHAPTER TEN

E arly sunlight filtered down through the boughs, dappling the loose stones of the pathway they rode over. The branches thinned, allowing more morning light to dribble through. It softened the edges of the trees so they appeared as little more than stoic guardians, benevolent and still. They had made it through.

"We are to meet with Elder Yarrow and his wife when we arrive shortly," Sorrell said, his voice rough and weary. "Do try to act respectful. We want to be accepted here."

They had not spoken the rest of the night, Sorrell's first words slipping past his lips as the darkness lifted. Hyacinth's cheek still throbbed, the bruises pulsing whenever she prodded the inside with her tongue. "Do we now?"

"I am an Elder, Hyacinth," he continued, clearing his throat. "Already accepted and revered. There are those who will look to me and know my words will keep them safe. You, my dear, will have to earn such treatment and are fortunate that I already have a step up here."

Hyacinth slipped her boots back on and dusted off the hem of her skirt. "As you say."

He turned and raised a hand to her face, smiling at the flinch it coaxed from her. "I do say, Hyacinth." He ran his thumb over the bruise. "Please remember that."

The carriage drew into the clearing, and Hyacinth's eyes widened as her new home came into view. It was not so unlike the village she left behind, the cottages small and thatched, bones dangling from the door. There was a stretch of earth in the center, scorched yellow as hers had been, and the remains of a feast still sat below the rising sun. Long tables with stained cloths and mismatched chairs, some overturned by the winds. The bunting of another poor girl hung high, the scraps of a life once lived and now something entirely different.

There was a strange dampness to the village, one that clung to Hyacinth, curling around her ankles in swathes of fine mist. She could smell the rain, though it had yet to fall from the heavy clouds above. Everything was muted, a wash of gray and brown, that even the trees seemed darker. Gulls screeched above her, scrawny creatures with tattered wings, diving to the ground to snatch at scraps. They tore at something, bent white feathers fluttering, twitching, beaks snapping. They peeled apart a smaller bird, its fluffy feathers stained red, its cries drowned out by the distant thrum of rolling water.

What lay beyond the village's edge was what inevitably caught Hyacinth's eye, sending a jolt through her all the way to her toes. Not far beyond the last cottage, it seemed as though the land simply ended. She could hear the roar of the winds, the crash of water, and a vast emptiness where woods should be.

"You are a sight to behold when spellbound, my dear," Sorrell said, stepping beside her, not quite touching but close enough. Too close. "The Great Deep."

"The forest has an end." Her voice was awed, a bare whisper snatched away by furious wind.

"Not an ending. A break perhaps, but do not let those waves deceive you. It begins again."

"How could you possibly know?"

"Because it is written." His words cut once more. "Because it is heresy to say otherwise, Hyacinth."

"What lies beneath the Deep—"

"The most hearty of welcomes to you both!"

A thunderous voice bounded across the green, belonging to a strange, small man, his mop of chestnut hair blowing wildly around his ruddy cheeks. "Blessed Oaks, you look weary! Come, come! I am Elder Yarrow." The man pressed a hand to his chest, taking a deep breath. "My deepest apologies; I had hoped to have met you right off the path, but I was waylaid. These villages will not run themselves."

"Indeed not." Sorrell gripped Elder Yarrow's hand as he thrust it toward him, looking momentarily bemused by his candor before he fixed his features. Hyacinth fought the smirk itching at her own lips. "I am Elder Reed from the second village to the east. This is my wife."

"My dear." Elder Yarrow plucked up her hand and pressed a wet kiss to the back. "The woods have indeed given us a rare bloom, I believe."

"You are too kind, sir," Hyacinth answered, feeling the warmth of his spittle trail over her skin.

"Mistress Yarrow will delight in your company, my dear. She'll have the kettle warming and fresh scones to fill your bellies!" Elder Yarrow pulled back his hand, his touch lingering a little too long on her wrist. She looked down where his plump fingers had wrapped around, noticing the streak of red left behind. "Come, warm your selves at our hearth, Elder Reed and Mistress Reed."

Hyacinth caught the sly lift of Sorrell's lip, the delight he held in her erasure. She wondered if she would have to fold her name away forever, tucking it into a pocket of herself that no one else could touch. She followed behind the two men in silence, biting her tongue hard enough to draw blood.

Elder Yarrow's cottage stood in the middle of the village, far from the cliff edge and the wild waters beyond. It was all white stone and ebony windowsills, pockmarked and crooked, its thatch a strange shade of brown, nothing like the golden roofs she had left behind.

Hyacinth ducked beneath the doorway to enter a dimly lit kitchen. The hearth fire barely warmed the space, the few candles dotted around doing little to lift the gloomy chill that seemed to seep in through the windows. Fish bones hung from the mantle, yellow and brittle looking. More dangled from above, woven alongside glass beads and little vials of sand and green.

"Seaweed from the water's edge," a soft voice drifted through the darkness. Mistress Yarrow stepped closer, wiping her hands on her apron. A brown scarf held back her flaxen hair, the fine strands at her face floating like a cobweb. Lines made a map of years on her skin, a tale of hardship. Hyacinth guessed she was a few years older than herself, not yet out of maidenhood. Her eyes were young, the brown soft. "To save us from the Teeth of the Deep, as well as those from the trees." She took hold of Hyacinth's hands, her skin cold. "You must also fill a bottle, Mistress Reed. Come down at dawn tomorrow, and I shall help you."

"I have never seen the Deep before," Hyacinth began, her eyes toward the churning sea, marveling at the expanse, stretching on and on and on. "It is a sight to behold."

"Look upon it with fear and humility, Mistress," Elder Yarrow warned, his tone pointed, eyes narrowed.

Hyacinth did not need to look to her husband to see the disdain on his face; she could feel it. She found pleasure in his discomfort and held it close.

"I shall look forward to our morning meeting, Mistress Yarrow," Hyacinth said, turning away from the men. She fixed her smile and tilted her head just so. A flare of light ignited in the other woman's eyes. It was barely an ember against the shadows on her pale face, but it was enough. "Now, I hear there are scones and tea?"

They settled at a table draped with fine lace cloth. The plates and teacups glimmered in shades of blue and green, a patchwork of colored glass worn smooth by the waves. They were lovely, delicate things that did not feel quite right against the surrounding gloom. The still-warm scones sat golden and plump between them, a slab of butter softened on a dish beside them. Tea was poured, the scent of chamomile soaking into the soot-clouded air. It was a war between the sweetness, the echoes of a home long gone yet unforgotten, and the heaviness, the smoke, and the lonely finality of life.

Hyacinth wanted the scents of the tea and the scones to overwhelm everything, but the smoke from the fire stung her eyes and made them water, and the tea was bitter and over-stewed.

"You'll have the cottage toward the back of the village," Elder Yarrow said around a mouthful of scone. "It needs a bit of work, but it'll make a fine family house in time."

"Who lived there before?" Hyacinth dabbed the crumbs from her lips and took another scone from the plate.

"Widow Fern." Mistress Yarrow scraped a thin layer of butter onto her scone before breaking it into small pieces. Not a morsel passed her lips. "Lost her husband to the trees a long while back. He was a Woodsman..."

"And strayed from the path!" Elder Yarrow's fist came banging down onto the table, shaking the teacups.

"We do not tolerate wickedness here," he said to Elder Reed. "He wandered, and he was devoured and left that poor woman to raise that filthy little harlot—"

"My dear! We have guests!"

"We are to live in a house seeped in sin?" Disgust curdled Sorrell's words. He coughed as though to hide it, but Hyacinth saw. "I trust it has been blessed, at least?"

"Blessed and re-carved, Elder Sir. No need to worry yourself." Elder Yarrow placed his fat hand over Sorrell's, patting it as though he were a child. "The house is good, the wood is good. I apologize if I startled you, Mistress Reed. I work tirelessly to keep this village safe, to keep the Teeth fed and away. I have the added Deep to fret after, you see, and it is no easy task. Widow Fern was a good woman, pious to the end, but her husband was one with drink...

with loose hands, Mistress, if you catch my meaning. Alas, his daughter was also one with a wandering eye, a wicked mouth, and loose legs."

Mistress Yarrow touched the circlet at her neck, its carvings nearly worn smooth. "She was such a pretty thing."

"Did you hang her, Elder Yarrow?" Hyacinth asked, placing her cold teacup back onto its saucer.

"She will go to the Deep, Mistress. The waters claim the women with sinful wants."

"Is that not a waste of bones?" Sorrell cut in with a quick glance to Hyacinth. She wondered if he imagined tossing her to the churning sea. Or would he rather watch the flames at her ankles? She could not quite tell.

"We keep the finger bones, Elder Reed." Elder Yarrow plucked another scone from the plate as casually as though discussing the weather rather than the dismemberment of unruly women.

"That is good to hear."

"The widow," Hyacinth began, feeling the scones lie heavy in her stomach. "She is..."

"Hanged under the last full moon. We have said our prayers, but you can keep her in yours if it comforts you."

"And the whore?" Sorrell added, leaning closer.

"The Deep will take her this eve," Elder Yarrow said. "As an Elder, you will be expected to be there. Listen to the words, Elder Reed, and remember them. It is perhaps not the welcome we would have wished to give you, but you know what must be done."

"Of course, I am eager to learn."

Too eager, thought Hyacinth, *to see a woman thrown to the waves.* As disgusted as she was by his indifference to human life, a part of her wanted to see what lay beneath the Deep. What horrors rested among the rock and weed, what new nightmares? Hyacinth still keenly felt the ache of her father's passing, of Abelia's death, their absences a bottomless void. She had little room left to feel much pity for a stranger. She couldn't let every sorrow in.

"We thank you for the good scones, Mistress Yarrow." Sorrell stood, curling one hand tightly over Hyacinth's shoulder. "But I would like to see myself and my wife settled before the evening draws in."

Mistress Yarrow nodded, the strained smile that creased her lips dipping. The scant light in her eyes also dimmed, a flicker dampened.

"I'll meet you in the morning," Hyacinth said, reaching across the white lace to take the pale hands of her new neighbor. "You'll have to teach me so much, I fear."

Her words were a fan to embers, and the smile returned. "I shall look forward to it, Mistress Reed."

CHAPTER ELEVEN

H yacinth's new home stood back from the others, closer to the trees. It was a crooked thing, its thatch in need of repair, its windowsills cracked. One of the panes of glass was broken, the shards sparkling in the wild grass that clung to the foundations. Some leaves had blown against the porch, the edges browning with autumn's tease. The cottage leaned toward the woods as she had done, a hand outstretched as though to feel the freedom of it.

"This is an insult," Sorrell hissed, peeling away some of the paint with a fingernail. "I deserve more than this...this shack!"

Hyacinth stepped onto the porch and touched the iron lantern on its hook. She had been the one to light the family lantern, the flicker of candlelight to guide her father home. She would light the one by her new door for the Woodsmen of her new home. Not for her husband, who would never set foot beyond the treeline.

"Do you think they knew of your...misgivings?" Hyacinth asked, not waiting for him to answer before she stepped inside.

"More likely your own, dear wife."

She turned. "Do you think so? That I have been more of an

influence here than you? To think, a Woodsman's daughter holding more sway than an Elder."

"They'll toss you to the waves," he threatened as he advanced, lips near hers, breathing the words into her lungs. "And I'll be sure to send your mother a fingertip."

"The trees or the Deep," she whispered, keeping her teeth behind her lips. "Such fortune have I."

Sorrell straightened, the loathing between them a vast, heady thing.

If the Teeth or the water's depths did not claim her, then surely the hate residing beneath her own roof would. It would be a slow death, a smothering of hope. A lingering suffocation.

"Ready the bed. I am weary."

Hyacinth did as she was bid, her body also exhausted, though her mind remained a whirl of bitter thoughts and a sense of home-sickness.

The bed was larger than any she had slept in before, bigger perhaps than even her parents had been. Tiny fish and sea snails had been carved into the four posts, the long tentacles of an octopus winding around the wood as though holding it up. The headboard was made from seaweed and coral. It was a beautiful thing, whimsical and soft, and she found it suited neither of them. The mattress was stuffed with straw, and it at least held firm, a solidness for her back. Hyacinth dressed it in the sheets she found in the cupboard, the scratchy fabric reminding her of home. She piled it with blankets knitted by hands unknown to her and tucked them in tight. From her bag, she pulled out the bones from her wedding, leaving one single fingerbone behind. She tied them to one of the posts, letting them clack against the wood.

"It will do." Sorrell came into the room, his face and hair damp from washing. His chest was bare, a smattering of pale, whispy hair curled over his skin. "You'll have to knit new coverings when the winter comes. These will not keep out the chill."

"I don't know how to knit."

"Then you will learn."

"Will you take the left or right side, dear husband, mine?"

He let out a laugh then, a snort that echoed sharply around the sparsely furnished space. "I will not sully myself to lie with a witch," he said, looking as though he were a breath away from spitting at her feet. "You are my penance, my shame eternal that only death will grant me respite from. I loathe you as much as you loathe me, my dear, and under this roof alone, we can forgo pretense."

Hyacinth stared in surprise.

He let out another derisive chuckle. "Are you so evil you would readily lie with the man who loosed the rope at your father's neck?"

She hit him, her hand rushing through the air without thought. Her palm stung, her eyes too. She willed the tears back, forbidding them to make tracks on her skin.

"May the trees be ever merciful to you, Elder Reed," she hissed. "For I will not be."

"My hand struck your face earlier today," Sorrell began, licking at the drop of blood on his lip. "And yours to mine this night, our feelings are shared. You are to sleep away from here, wife. You are not to lay your hand upon me again, do you understand?"

"If you understand the same!" she returned.

"Away with you." He flicked his hand before climbing into the bed. "You foul thing."

Hyacinth made her way back down the creaky stairs to the old moth-eaten sofa beside the fireplace. The pale blue velvet had faded, the seams split in places to allow the stuffing to leak out. It was no wider and no narrower than her bed at home, and she found that as she fell into sleep, her hand reached out against the expanse of space where her sisters would have been. The loneliness dug in against her ribs, curled there, and settled, leaving little room for anything else.

Darkness covered everything, a heavy black, unlike anything Hyacinth had encountered before. She felt it in her lungs, a cold expanse of nothingness. Footsteps echoed clumsily on the stairs. There was a curse, a low muttering, and a soft thud.

"The matches, woman!" Sorrell called out, his voice close to her feet. "Light the damned candles and make haste."

Hyacinth rose, shaking off the heaviness of slumber. Her feet found the splayed hand of her husband, and she trod down firmly, breathing in his hiss of pain. She lit one lonely candle, thinning out the dark.

"Get your cloak. We must not be late."

"I have never seen an offering of bone at this hour," Hyacinth said, slipping on her boots and warm cloak. She paid little attention to her hair, feeling it tangle around her face.

"We are not to question the reasoning of our betters..."

"Perhaps we should."

He spun, having dusted himself off, his face red with indignation. She could see his ire through the candlelight, enjoying how the flame caught his shame-tinged cheeks. "I bid you be silent. Just stand and watch with the other women. Whisper your prayers and bow your head."

"Of course."

He did not comment on the bite in her words but pushed her aside as he stepped from the cottage.

Hyacinth followed, feeling the chill of the briny late-night air sting her cheeks.

Lanterns lit the way, held aloft by silent hands. Hyacinth unhooked the one that hung from their porch and fell in step with the villagers she had yet to speak to. They did not walk down to the water's edge. Instead, they followed a winding path upwards through thin-boughed trees and long grass.

The sound of waves roared over the quiet night, water crashing against the rocks as though seeking to devour them. Hyacinth had never been so close to the sea, had never heard it, smelled it, or tasted such saltiness in the air. Curiosity inched her forward to the

THE BONE DRENCHED WOODS

space where the land ended and the sky began, her mouth open, eyes wide. A soft tug at her arm drew her back.

"We'll not have you going over, Mistress Reed," Mistress Yarrow said, fingers curling in the fabric of Hyacinth's cloak. "I fear you will be missed."

Hyacinth looked behind her to her husband in his mask and the other Elders standing still and watchful. She didn't think anyone there would shed a tear if she toppled over the edge.

"Are you to throw that poor girl off the cliff?" Hyacinth couldn't see the widow's daughter, could hear no screams or pleas, no begging for salvation or mercy.

"Come with me, my dear. Come stand with us."

Hyacinth allowed herself to be led away, to stand to the side of the Elders with the other wives. They smiled at her, hands brushing against her shoulders as though to comfort her. It was a strange thing to be coddled at someone else's misfortune.

"You are to watch," one woman began, the streaks of gray in her hair bright in the moonlight. "Remain close to us if you wish, but you must watch, Mistress Reed."

And watch, she did.

In silence, they brought out the widow's daughter, bound tight. With the torchlight surrounding her, Hyacinth could see the dirt on her skin and the bloodied bandages around her hands where two of her fingers had been taken. No sound escaped lips sewn roughly with black thread so no more wickedness could fall from her tongue. They would have done so with Emory Merrow if she had not run.

No one spoke the young woman's name, and Hyacinth wished she had asked for it. The widow's daughter would go to the Deep and be forgotten, bones taken, and name left to drift. Not a death but an extinction.

"Let your bones keep us, as the Deep will keep you." Elder Yarrow stepped forward, arms stretched wide, his voice almost swallowed up by the roar of the waves. "Let your sins be drowned."

"Drown our sins," Hyacinth echoed the words, feeling them as empty and useless as the ones she had uttered before.

With a great creaking, a wooden platform was wheeled to the edge of the cliff. It looked not unlike a hanging platform, but instead of a noose, it bore a hook. It pierced her skin with ease, slipping through muscle and missing the bone so it clung tight. There was little blood, just enough to stir those below. The widow's daughter writhed, her back arching so she slid further down the hook. With her dark hair whipping wildly around her, she looked so much like Briony. The thought of her sisters hanging there, dangling from ragged flesh, made Hyacinth's blood cold. They were always a breath away from the pyre, the noose, and the hook; one wrong word, one rumor, and they would be snatched away. Would she feel it, she wondered, so far away from any of them? Would the word of their deaths reach her so far through the trees? Or would they die nameless, like the widow's daughter, thrown to hungry mouths in some strange village away from home?

Hyacinth strained her neck, looking beyond the widow's daughter to the dark shapes swirling through the waves. They were colossal shadows, a deep blackening of the waters, silent and terrible. She wanted to see, needed to see.

Wheels groaned, the rope loosening to lower the hook down and down and down. The stitches at the girl's lips popped, a soundless cry bleeding through torn lips. They had taken her tongue, too. Down she went, squirming and bending, until the waters rushed over her legs, her chest, down her silent throat.

Hyacinth stared down into the churning pitch, seeing nothing but the rolling waters...but she heard Them. The creaking of giant jaws stretching wide, the noise reverberating over the waves. Teeth snapped as loud as a thunderclap; if they tore into each other or the widow's daughter, Hyacinth had no way of knowing. The lantern light rippled over the waves but not beneath, and Hyacinth could only make out vague shapes in the blackness. Then she saw it. The widow's daughter had been stripped clean, her flesh sloughed from her bones.

The hook was lifted, the rope frayed, edges catching the wind to flutter like hair. Nothing else remained. The Deep stilled, its shadows slipping further under until there was only the thrash of white-tipped water sounding against the rock.

CHAPTER TWELVE

Hyacinth slipped from the cottage at first light, her bones aching and her temper strained. She had slept fitfully on the sofa, blankets tangled around her legs, her feet binding her tight as though preparing her for the waves. There was a different brutality to the Deep, one she had not been ready for. The horrors of the Teeth were embedded into her bones, her soul. Her muscles knew how to react. Her body did not yet know how to twist around the knowing of the Deep, and it ached.

The fire was little more than ashes when she woke, the warmth long gone. Hyacinth did not move to rekindle it, though not because of a lack of skill. Her husband could find the wood and the matches, or they would both be cold.

The morning brought with it a cloudless sky, the early autumnal sun reaching low over the treetops. From her porch, she could see the calm blue ocean, its waves slumbering, lapping with a gentle roll in the distance. It bore so little of the previous night's rolling turmoil. She wondered if the Deep slept, like the trees. If they were ever sated and full, or if their hunger was endless.

If there was something else beyond the vast waters, like her father had told her, she could not fathom it.

"Mistress Reed." The call drifted across the clearing, as soft as fog. "I could hardly sleep. I was so keen to see you again."

Mistress Yarrow skipped down the narrow pathway that interlocked all the houses, her hands clutching a tin cup. She wore a dress as pale as seafoam, her cream apron embroidered with little shining shells tied neatly at her waist. Her hair was bound in a scarf, her golden strands held back firmly so none could escape.

"Good morning. Please, I beg you. Call me Hyacinth." She outstretched her hand as the woman thrust the cup toward her.

"You seemed to like the tea yesterday," Mistress Yarrow explained, nodding to the cup. "I was unsure of what supplies you might have, and you really cannot start the day without a cup of tea, Mistress Reed."

"Hyacinth."

"Hush now, none of that." Mistress Yarrow waited until Hyacinth had sipped the bitter tea before taking her free hand. "Now, I don't know what frivolities you enjoyed in your old village, but it is not like that here. You need to be careful. Everything is always so very hungry here."

The warning came quick and sharp, hissed from thinned lips.

"I understand," she replied, forcing herself to take another sip of tea.

"Do you?" The words were firm. "Because you must, Mistress Reed. You must."

Still holding onto her cup, Hyacinth followed the woman down the path toward the cliff's edge, where the waves below rolled against the stones. Lifting her skirts, Mistress Yarrow descended a curving set of stone steps. There was nothing to grip onto. The stone was wet with moss and worn smoothly with age. She need not have worried Sorrell would feed her to the Deep; she was sure to break her neck instead.

"Hold on, my dearest."

"To what?"

Mistress Yarrow huffed a laugh. "The other women will join us later. I thought it best we come early so I can show you what needs doing, or else you might get in the way."

Hyacinth did not answer, too focused on where her feet were planted to engage in conversation. Where she staggered and fumbled down the steps, Mistress Yarrow skipped over them with ease.

The shoreline was a thin, winding stretch of stone and sand and slick green. Old seaweed lay tangled against the jagged corners of the rocks, baked in the summer heat and left to rot through autumn. There was a sharp, pungent smell to it all, though it wasn't unpleasant.

"Mr. Carroway!" Mistress Yarrow called out, her feet landing firmly on the wet pebbles. Hyacinth scrambled behind, skirt in one hand, empty teacup in the other. "Are the fish in?"

"You're a bloody hour early, Yarrow!" Came the sharp reply, though Hyacinth could not see who it belonged to.

"Watch your tongue!" Mistress Yarrow scolded as she hitched up her skirts, the shallow waters threatening her feet. "We have newcomers to the village, which you would have known if you had turned up at the last meet. This is Mistress Reed, wife of our new Elder."

Wooden crates and nets lay scattered over the stones, some piled high where the voice echoed. There were old fishing hooks and tools lying on flat rocks, small wooden boxes stacked with bottles filled with green weed, and knotted rope that had blacked and frayed stretching out towards the waves. If there was any order to it, Hyacinth could not tell.

The stench of fish brought tears to Hyacinth's eyes, the smell wet and oily. She had grown used to the tang of blood, of deer meat and offal, but the briny fish with their gleaming scales and white eyes made her stomach sour. She swallowed quickly, then breathed deeply through her mouth.

"Can you debone a fish?" A head appeared from behind a large box of salt. He was young and tan, a riot of copper curls lying in tangles across his face.

"I beg your pardon?" Hyacinth placed her cup between the pebbles, planting her feet so she didn't stumble. The waves crept close to her boots, the spray hitting her skirts and dampening her stockings. Could it taste her? The Deep, as she stood close enough to smell the salt, the brine, the green of the choking weeds clinging to the rock.

"Can you gut a fish, filet it, and keep its bones?"

Hyacinth lifted her head, meeting Mr. Carroway's gray eyes. Her lip curled at his tone as though she were lesser.

"Not a fish, sir," she answered, feet crunching over the stones to look closer into the baskets. "But I've cleaned my fair share of game. I doubt it is much different." Hyacinth hoped she would grow used to the stink of them and that her tongue would soon like the taste. She never much liked going hungry.

"Needs to be done before the tide comes in."

"Down here?"

He grinned back at her, showing teeth. "You'll get no help lugging the crates up the steps, Mistress."

Mistress Yarrow placed a gentle hand on her shoulder, a kindness that seeped into Hyacinth like a sponge to water. "We tie the bones in a fourth knot and bind in the middle, three bones below. You know your carvings?"

"I do. My father taught me well."

The woman nodded, her smile turning tight. "I am sure he did."

Hyacinth was handed a knife, and a crate of fish was pushed before her. They stared at her, their filmy eyes wide and empty, their gaping mouths bloodied. They had been caught with nets and bludgeoned, given a quick death. One far more merciful than the one bestowed onto the widow's daughter, Hyacinth thought.

Mr. Carroway busied himself with hauling in his nets, and Mistress Yarrow settled herself on a rock and began to slice her blade through the glistening skin of a fish.

"We do this thrice a week unless the Deep is hungry—if it has not been sated. The Woodsmen see to the trees, as I am sure you are familiar with. The Boatman see to the waters."

"Are you a Boatman, Mr. Carroway?" Hyacinth asked, slipping the skin from her fish with ease. She placed the filets into a salted box beside her and made a pile of the wet bones at her feet.

"Am I fuck!"

"May the Oak and the Brine give you mercy!" Mistress Yarrow hissed, highly offended. She pointed the tip of her blade toward Mr. Carroway. "Did you not learn from last time?"

"Will you tell, Mistress?" It sounded like a dare, his words meant to antagonize.

"You ought to be mindful," was her answer, and Hyacinth had no knowing of what it meant.

Mr. Carroway cocked his head, grin unwavering, eyes too bright. "Will you tell, Mistress Reed?"

She looked up from her fish, hands streaked with gore. "I am not in the habit of sending a man to a whipping, sir. No matter the foulness of his tongue."

"Then I am your servant this day, Mistress Reed."

"What does my silence gain me, Mr. Carroway?" Mistress Yarrow asked, still on the third fish, Hyacinth noted, whereas she was on her sixth.

"I shall let you know when the tide is due, Mistress," he answered, tossing more fish into the crates of salt. "Save your pretty skin from those beneath."

The women from the village arrived when the sun rose higher than the hilltops, its rays glistening over the waters. They joined them, holding skirts and knives and rope, settling on the rocks beside Hyacinth.

They brought with them baskets of food and gossip, welcoming Hyacinth with warm smiles, passing her pieces of browned apple cake and elderflower tonic. She ate and drank with fish blood on her hands, watching as the others did the same.

She had never involved herself with the villagers before, preferring to stay in the company of her sisters and Abelia. There was something almost comforting about being surrounded by the smiles and quick hands of the other women as if they did not see something wicked in her, something wrong.

"Where will the fish go?" Hyacinth asked, laying the tender flesh, freshly stripped, into the salt. "Surely not all of these will go to the Deep?"

"One crate will be taken back to the village," Mistress Yarrow explained, a small pile of fishbones at her feet. "It will be enough to feed our bellies. Do not worry, Mistress Reed, we'll not have you starve. The others will be loaded onto the boats for the Boatmen to take out to the Deep."

"And it keeps Them away?"

The small knife in Mistress Yarrow's hand stilled. "Most of the time, yes."

"Until they still come."

"Enough of that." The knife pointed at Hyacinth, the tip close to her skin. "If all is good, if we remain good, it will be enough."

Hyacinth nodded, forcing a smile.

Mistress Yarrow lowered her knife and went back to slicing her fish.

"How far do the Boatmen sail out?" Hyacinth pressed, etching lines into wet bone.

"Past the horizon. Do you see where the waters darken out there? Beyond that point, they go, laden with fish and with prayers on their tongues."

Hyacinth nodded. The tension between them lifted, and she continued her tasks with little more to say. At one moment, she paused while the other women chattered, her knife deep in the belly of a silver-scaled fish, and tried to listen. She waited for a song, a call, the echoes of women lost beneath the dark waters, like those from the woods, from the trees. The waves rolled in, whispering against the rocks, but nothing called to her.

"The Boatmen are coming," Mrs. Aster said, leaning close to Hyacinth's ear. She was an older woman, hair fully gray, her brown skin creased by years at the shore beneath the sun. "See, there's my husband. Does he not look fine?"

Mr. Aster led the Boatmen down, dressed in deep blue and green, the color of stormy seas. He raised his hand in greeting before slipping his mask over his lined face. They were not masks of hare skin but of birds. White and gray feathers spread out from a curving beak, the edges of them frayed and broken. Some of the younger Boatmen had beaks of pure yellow, pristine, and sharp. Hyacinth wondered how many times they had been sent out onto the waters and how long it would take for them to take on the haggard look of the others.

"The tide grows near," Mr. Carroway called, pulling up his nets. "Get the lot on the boats and take the rest up."

"Come, Mistress Reed, you've done well. Let us stop for tea." Mistress Yarrow wiped her hands on her pretty apron, streaking it with more blood and fish guts.

"Delightful." Hyacinth dragged her own hands down her skirts, feeling the pieces of bone fragments stick behind her fingernails.

Hyacinth watched the water while the other women made their way back up the worn steps, straining her eyes to see past the shallows, where it darkened and seemed to go on forever.

The Boatmen took their boxes of salted fish, tied the knotted bones to their belts, and with their strange, feathered masks, they pushed out into the Deep.

Hyacinth realized Mistress Yarrow waited alongside her.

"The Woodsmen keep the paths clear," she began. "They keep the village free of the trees and the Teeth within. The Boatman... what paths are they keeping clear?"

"There used to be boats, Mistress," Mr Carroway whispered. He glanced toward Mistress Yarrow as though waiting for her to stop him. "Boats as big as clouds, able to carry a hundred—a thousand people to beyond the Deep. But the people grew greedy, and the Deep grew hungry. It pulled them down, pulled the land down, and it ate, and it ate, and it ate..."

"Enough!" Mistress Yarrow snatched Hyacinth's hand, her fingers still slick with innards. "There is nothing beyond the Deep,

Morgan Carroway, nothing in those waters except a long and painful death. An eternal death, as the trees, as the Deep."

"As you say." He nodded to the boats making their way out across the water. "They will go out far beyond the horizon to dump our scant offerings in the hope that our village will be spared. That the waters will not rise up to swallow us all."

A hopelessness weighed down on Hyacinth, taking with it any good feeling the morning had brought. "Are we truly little more than delectable flesh to ancient beings with insatiable appetites?"

"Bless the Oaks and bless the Deep," Mistress Yarrow said, her hand going to the circle at her neck. "We are fortunate, Mistress Reed, are we not? That they stay away."

There was no room given to answer, no room to argue, so Hyacinth nodded as though she agreed. As though she were happy to simply exist and wait to die, or be eaten.

She accepted neither.

CHAPTER THIRTEEN

W ith her hands and clothing reeking of fish guts, Hyacinth departed from the other women, the promise she would stop for tea still clinging to her chapped lips. She remembered the times in her village when the Elders' wives would gather for tea and picnics, sitting still and somber like obedient pups. She and Abelia would watch, giggling behind their hands, their muffled snorts stolen up by the winds and whisked away. They were never caught, not once. The looming trees seemed to swallow their mirth, the fragments of joy, and kept it hidden.

What would Abelia think of her now with her stained hands and borrowed name?

The seaside village was larger than the one she grew up in, the crooked houses leaning in closer, their windows glazed with colored sea glass. Pebbles coated the outside walls, black and brown and yellow, all covered in a thin layer of green moss. The paint on most of the houses was curling and old. Hyacinth wondered if the closeness of the waters ate a little at the doorways, the windowsills. That, no matter the bones sent out, the Deep would still take, bit by bit. Would it take them all in the end? Would it matter?

Feeling the stickiness of her hands dry in the late morning sun,

Hyacinth quickened her pace back to her cottage, longing for clean water and soap. Clouds thickened overhead, gray bleeding through the blue. The air grew heavy with the threat of rain. She hoped their roof wouldn't leak or that if it did, it would trickle down onto her husband and leave her dry below.

Hyacinth heard the sound of footsteps before she saw it, a soft rustling in dry leaves. She paused, her eyes following the shadow. She was close to the trees, close to her cottage, darkness and shadow blending in a tapestry of pitch. She reached for her circlet, feeling the carvings marked out by her father's deft fingers. No prayers sprang to her tongue, although she rooted for them; a curse fell instead, sharp and clear.

"Get the fuck away from my door!" Hyacinth stomped her foot, gulping down fear. "I'll not become a feast for hollow hearts on my own threshold. Be gone!"

Something wavered, darkness stretching up. The trees shook, rattling the bones. She swore she could hear the distant bells of laughter. There was a brush against her legs, a solid thing, and she screamed.

It growled back, teeth bared and hackles up.

Hyacinth stilled, a hand at her chest, the thud of her heart against her palm. "You awful creature!" She fought not to strike it, but though she did not raise her fist, the dog flinched, its ears back and head sinking low. Hyacinth softened. "You wicked thing."

It was a huge beast of a dog, its head near her shoulder. Wiry gray fur stuck up in all directions, threaded through with silver. Despite its size, it cowered, completely silent after its growl. It turned from Hyacinth to peer back into the dark woods. Hyacinth stepped forward, one hand stretched out to seek its coarse coat, feeling its solidness, its company. She saw nothing through the trees, no shift of shadow or turn of earth. The branches wavered only slightly, the bones silent.

"Was it you in the woods?" She crouched down to scratch behind his ears. It happily leaped forward, shoving Hyacinth to the ground to climb into her lap.

"You daft brute," she said with a laugh. She continued to pet the animal, its weight against her a welcome comfort. Like the crush of arms, a sleeping sibling warming your bed, a body in the grass curled tight. "I cannot keep you."

"You cannot think to bring that foul beast in here!"

The outrage on her husband's face was a gift, and Hyacinth tucked the moment away deep inside where he could not see it.

"It looks as though a devil has spat it out!"

The choice to allow the dog into her home had not entirely been Hyacinth's. She had made several attempts to push the stubborn creature away, to force it back to wherever it had ventured from. It was unmoving, a solid lump of refusal. It kept close on her walk back, a shadow at her feet.

"If you are accusing our fellow neighbors of harboring demons, dear husband, may I suggest you take it to the Council. It may yet belong to someone," Hyacinth said, placing a bowl of fresh water before the dog. "Though I would be certain of its possession before you embarrass yourself and offend our neighbors."

The dog quickly lapped the water, then looked up at her with mournful black eyes. For its size, it seemed far too skinny, and Hyacinth wondered how long it had been in the woods. With every movement Hyacinth made, it moved too, never more than a breath away. It cared not that she was sharp-tongued and ill-mannered, that there was a wickedness to her. If it could taste her sins on its black tongue, it did not seem to mind. It accepted her in a way even her sisters had not. Only Abelia. Abelia had seen her.

"I will have nothing to do with it." Sorrell spat, appraising the dog in the same way he looked upon her. "I will not! It is yours to do with as you wish, but you are to keep away from me!"

Hers. Hers alone. Gratitude slipped against her mouth before she swallowed it down. "Have you a meeting to be ready for?"

"I am well enough prepared for tonight," he answered, slipping into her armchair. "It is exciting, wife, to be welcomed into the fold. You should be thankful for it."

"Are you?"

He stared through her, eyes cold and lips hard. "I will be."

Hyacinth turned to the window, looking through the cracked glass to the wild Deep beyond the small, broken cottage. "I feel there is a savagery to this place," she said. "One I think will suit you just fine."

"I believe you are right." Sorrell stretched out his legs, smiling broadly. "I wonder how you will fare here, dear wife."

"There is a place for me here with the other Elder wives," Hyacinth said, hand slowly moving up and down the broad neck of her new companion. "I could slip into that role with ease. Keep all eyes away from me, blend in. Let no one hear the wickedness from my tongue."

"And will you?"

"Maybe."

He sat forward to peer at her. "Do you seek to threaten me, then? To drag my name into the dirt along with your morals?"

Hyacinth shrugged, her focus remaining on the dog. "I simply wish to make it clear that we could easily be one another's ruin and that if I fall, I shall be taking you with me."

Sorrell stood, long-limbed and fair, like a stalk of wheat. Beside her, the dog let out a low growl, hackles rising.

"You are late to tea, my dear," Sorrell said, keeping his simmering anger contained. "It would be a shame for you to displease your new friends. I fear it could be awfully lonely here."

He walked away, his heavy boot steps echoing on the bare wood floors, leaving her to stand alone with her sticky hands and blood-stained dress. Though not quite alone. She gave the dog another quick scratch behind the ears before fetching a clean dress from her trunk. With a bowl of cool water and a bar of waxy soap, she cleaned herself by the fire, scrubbing at her skin as though to wash the weight of her husband's words away.

Unlike Hyacinth's cottage, the Drove stood close to the cliff's edge, its foundation clinging to the rock as though reminding those inside that they were always within reach of the Deep. Carvings of sea creatures with huge maws were etched into the beams, yellowing fish bones hung from the windows and doorways, and the flagstones underfoot were stained deep black in places where blood had fallen. It was an awful, sacred place.

Hyacinth sat beside Mistress Yarrow to the side of the hall, their bench dressed with long velvet cushions, unlike the bare wood seating for the other villagers. She had forced down a cup of bitter tea and some scones, sitting in polite silence while the other women stitched banners made of clothing for some child's name day.

"You will fall into a routine in no time," Mistress Yarrow assured her, leaning close so her voice did not echo. "Better an Elder's wife than a Woodsman's, or Oaks forgive me, a Boatman's."

"My father was a Woodsman," Hyacinth haughtily replied, uncaring of the reaction her words might cause.

"And I suppose your mother stood waiting under the porch light each night for his return?"

"What of it?"

"You will never have to fear that your husband will not return to you. Be thankful, Mistress Reed. There is less burden on your heart."

Hyacinth forced a lovely smile on her face, making her cheeks ache. Briony would have been happy with the life thrust on her, the chance to be overly pious and ridiculous to others; she would have slipped within the folds of the Elder wives with ease.

A hush slipped over the Form as the Elders took their places at the front, up on a dais, so they overlooked all. They each wore their masks of scale and fin, the edges rotted, eye cavities blackened with age. Hyacinth spotted Sorrell sitting in the center, head held high and proud. He broke her gaze first, and she turned with a smile, soft and lovely and devious.

From the crowd, she noted Morgan Carroway watching her, taking in the little smile on her lips, her evident disdain for her husband. She glared back, lips falling, eyes hard, until he, too, turned away.

"Well met!" Elder Yarrow called out, voice booming across the quiet. "The Hunger is content, my friends, my neighbors. It sleeps."

A collective murmur shuddered through the Form, the whispered prayers blending with the scraping of wood. Hands touched the carvings on the benches, the pendants at throats. It was a sigh of tentative relief.

"But we are not to be complacent!" Elder Yarrow continued. "The Teeth are always there, always waiting. They hunger for our sins, for the sins of our children, and we carve the bones to keep them safe."

"We carve the bones," Hyacinth murmured the words with the others, feeling strange uttering them while sitting on a velvet cushion and not on the benches with her family.

"They feed on wickedness," Elder Yarrow said, pausing to cast his masked gaze over the Form. "On the weakness of the flesh. We do all we can to sate their appetites, but we must also sate our own! Our temptations and vices, and those of our neighbors—we remove the rot from within to keep us safe. And we feed the Deep."

Same sermon, different hall. Hyacinth had heard all the words and warnings before, had sat and watched those brought forward, their sins heavy on their tongues, their penance sharp and unforgiving.

Another Elder stood, his mask of scales catching the early morning light. He was taller, leaner, almost spider-like in the way he moved, the way he watched.

"Elder Lichen," whispered Mistress Yarrow in her ear. "It is wise not to catch his attention."

"Let those warnings into your hearts and souls and keep them there," Elder Lichen said, his thin voice stretching over those who listened. "But also, welcome to our newest family, an honored Elder from one of the eastern villages, Elder Reed and his Wife. May we welcome you, too, into our hearts and souls and keep you there."

There came some polite applause and a few murmurs of welcome. More whispers were uttered behind raised hands. What rumors had followed them, Hyacinth knew not.

"There will be a feast," Mistress Yarrow said, words tickling Hyacinth's ear. "A dance to welcome you to our village. They are only held when a new Elder comes, and it has been so long, I cannot wait."

"Who did Elder Reed replace?" Hyacinth whispered back.

"Elder Hewn." The reply was so quiet that despite feeling the words against her cheek, Hyacinth scarcely heard them. "They came at night after the Woodsman made safe the paths. They still came. The bones and the marks were not enough. They took Elder Hewn and twelve others."

"The trees?"

"Aye, Mistress. The Deep, too."

Hyacinth straightened in her seat, reminded that they were not safe even when they said their prayers, carved their bones, did everything asked of them. That she had not only the Teeth to fear but also the Deep. She was trapped, caged in by hungry mouths and awful men.

"What was left behind?" Hyacinth whispered, noting the glances of the other wives looking her way.

Mistress Yarrow stared ahead, her hands clasped neatly in her lap, the perfect, pious mistress. "The Teeth left nothing but fragments of bone and roots," she whispered. "The Deep—it peeled back skin, like we do with the fishes. It did not eat them."

"Do my words bore you, Mistress Yarrow?" Elder Lichen asked, his fingers clenched over the wooden pulpit he stood behind. His eyes gleamed from beneath his mask, the scales a pale, shimmering green. They blackened at the edges, slowly rotting. "What wisdom do you deem unworthy for all to hear?"

Mistress Yarrow stood. "You have my apologies. I only thought to ensure Mistress Reed knew of our stories, our past..."

"And gossip?"

"No gossip, Elder Lichen." Mistress Yarrow placed a hand on Hyacinth's shoulder. "Mistress Reed is unfamiliar with the Deep. She needs to know of its dangers—its appetites."

Elder Lichen turned his scaled face toward Hyacinth. "What do you think of the Deep, Mistress Reed? Do you fear it as you should fear the Teeth?"

"I do, Elder Sir," Hyacinth replied. "I fear it more so."

"Do you now?" Elder Lichen smiled, stretching the mask across his face. Hyacinth could see the gleam of brine beneath the scales. All the masks were wet, trickling over the wearer's skin like oil.

"Shall we continue?" Elder Yarrow demanded, casting a furious gaze toward his wife. "Sit down and be silent!"

His wife quietly complied.

He turned back to Hyacinth. "Mistress Reed, you are to bestow your husband with his new mask and keep your idle chatter behind your lips. Am I clear?"

Hyacinth stepped up to the dais without another word. A box was presented to her, velvet-lined and edged in pearl. A mask sat inside, the white scales speckled in blood. It was wet like the others, but it had a freshness to it, no signs of decay. Hyacinth plucked it from the black velvet, the fleshy underside tacky to her fingers. It still bore its eyes, thin globules of white that would be nearly impossible to see out of. They would have to rot first.

"We welcome you, Elder Reed," Elder Yarrow called out, pushing past Elder Lichen to stand at the pulpit. "Feed the Deep."

Sorrell stepped up, chin lifted, shoulders back. Hyacinth wanted to tell him how ridiculous he looked, but she kept her tongue.

"Feed the Deep," Sorrell echoed.

Hyacinth slipped the mask over his face, feeling him flinch as the cold, bloodied skin touched his cheeks. There was no silk ribbon to fasten it but a twist of fishing line and gut. It sliced against Hyacinth's fingers, drawing a trickle of blood. Red slithered down Sorrell's skin, mingling with the thick brine.

"Don't stumble back to your seat." Hyacinth leaned in close, the stench of fish assaulting her senses. "You wouldn't want to embarrass yourself."

His fingers brushed against hers, almost frantically searching for something to hold on to. Hyacinth pulled away, wiping her bloodied finger over her skirt. Sorrell wavered, unable to see through the dead eyes of his mask, but he did not fall. She wished she had tripped him, sent him sprawling to the ground before the other Elders.

Hyacinth left the Drove with the other wives, breathing in the salty air as she stepped outside. She let them go ahead, hanging back so she stood at the cliff's edge, her skirts billowing in the wind, hair wild around her face. Below, the waves crashed against the rock, taking more and more of the cliffside with every cascade. The gulls screeched overhead, the air thick with a chorus of their screams and rolling water. What would Abelia have made of it, of the stretch of dark waters, the white of the surf, the endlessness of it all? Hyacinth felt so small, standing at the edge, with the Teeth at her back and the Deep before her. A morsel for something hungry, like Abelia had been, like the widow's daughter writhing and bleeding, a maggot on a hook, and little more.

With the others gone and with the wind beating at her face, Hyacinth screamed over the abyss. The sound was snatched away instantly, lost to the waters, swallowed up as if she had never made a sound.

CHAPTER FOURTEEN

E venings grew into a lonely repetition of her husband's cold
companionship, their stilted silences filling the barren
rooms along with woodsmoke and dampness. Hyacinth
slept on the sofa, listening to the sounds of the Woodsmen as they
traveled back to their homes. She could hear the wind in the trees,
the rattle of bones. The dog curled up beside her, lending warmth,
his giant frame almost squashing her completely, though she found
she minded little. She had begun to call him Faolan, her own little
wolf, whose great tail would thump beside her when she did. If he
approved of the name or just liked the sound of her voice, she
didn't know, but it didn't matter.

No one came forward to claim him, so he remained. Sorrell did
not question who she asked, nor did he ask how hard she sought to
send the creature on his way, so she did not need to lie. The cottage
took on the dog's scent, mingling with the dampness already there.
Patches of thick drool stained her skirts, the pillow where she laid
her head, no longer alone.

Hyacinth and Sorrell passed one another like ghosts during the
day with the occasional barbed word and subtle threat, their

tension kept at bay by the ever-present dog. He started to accompany her along with her daily chores, happy to follow as she took her leave each morning.

Hyacinth made her way along the twisting pathways, boots crunching on the fallen leaves. The air grew colder, fogging her breath. It would not be long before the first frosts came; winter always brought with it a different sort of hunger. There was a silence to its nights that had Hyacinth lying awake in her bed, matching her breath to that of her sisters. She would listen, and the nights would be still, frost creeping against the windows. Nothing would sing, nothing would call. But in those heavy mornings, on the frost-tipped grass, there would be bones and torn flesh, tendrils of cold-damaged vines, and the curl of delicate petals.

The blood always looked so much brighter in winter.

With her basket hooked over one arm, Hyacinth wandered close to the edge of the trees, keeping both feet out from beneath their shadows. The leaves had turned shades of orange and red, and piles of them lay scattered, drifting into the village, bringing color to the surrounding hues of brown and gray. She plucked blackberries from the bushes, being mindful of the thorns, and tossed a few into her mouth, enjoying the burst of sweetness. There were more further in; there always was. Huge brambles covered in fat berries that would make the best jam, the best cordial. She and Celandine had once snuck through the branches just beyond their village, snatching up handfuls of berries before they were caught and dragged back by their mother. Hyacinth could still feel the smack if she closed her eyes, hear the way it echoed. The basket had been forced out of her small hands and tossed into the woods, the juices splattering over the new frost like blood.

Faolan remained at her side, nose in the bushes, eyes staring straight into the woods. He made no sound, nor did he give a sign that anything was watching them back. Hyacinth plucked the last few berries with her stained hands, and with her basket full, she turned for home.

"You, girl!"

The shout startled Hyacinth, and she tightened her grip on her basket, one hand finding and digging into Faolan's wiry coat.

"Get you here, girl!"

If no one used her name, Hyacinth was certain she would forget the sound of it entirely. Fog had begun to roll across the ground, weaving its way around Hyacinth's legs. There was the crunch of leaves, the heavy sound of boots.

"Who is there?" Hyacinth called out. She loosened her hold on the dog, and he stepped in front of her, his black lips curled.

"I will not stop him if he decides to bite—who are you?"

"Found that cursed beast, aye?" An old man stepped from beyond the trees, leaning heavily on a twisted bough. A string of teeth had been tied to the top, some yellowing, some cracked. Some were still fresh and bloodied. "Or did he find you, girl?"

Hyacinth stepped back, her basket clutched tight to her middle. "Why are you in the woods? You look like no Woodsman I have seen before."

"There were bones to be hung. A dainty finger bone added to a knot of weed and hair." The old man leaned on his stick, one hand outstretched to wriggle his thin and crooked fingers. His eyes moved from Hyacinth to the dog at her side. "I had time on my hands, you see, and I like them to be kept busy. Now, tell me why you are so close to the Teeth, girl?"

"Picking blackberries."

The old man laughed, the sound like sawdust. "With that hound, eh? People will talk."

"And what will they say, Mr..."

"Mr. Douglas, Mistress Reed." The old man held out a weathered hand, and Hyacinth took it, feeling his dry skin scrape across hers. Faolan's hackles relaxed, but he kept his eyes trained on the man before her.

"It don't take much to get tongues wagging here, Mistress, and I guess you know that. A girl so close to the trees with a wildling hound at her side, they've punished folk for less."

"He is just a dog."

Mr. Douglas nodded. "And you are just a girl. Matters little to most folk here, though. Mind which shadows you walk over, Mistress Reed."

"I am more than capable of looking after myself, but I thank you for your concern," Hyacinth said, swinging her basket back onto one arm.

She heard the old man follow behind her back to the village, his footsteps slow and heavy. She did not look back.

"You still have no talent for knitting," Mistress Yarrow said, plucking the needles and tangle of wool from Hyacinth's hands. "I insist you stop before you strangle yourself."

She sat in the Drove with the other Elder wives, Mistress Yarrow at her side. Faolan lay at her feet, and although she received a few raised eyebrows, no one spoke of him. Small chatter wound around the clicking of needles, a peaceful way to spend a morning. But Hyacinth's hands ached with frustration. Needlework had never been her calling.

"I beg of you, find me something else to do." Hyacinth laughed, echoing the smile on Mistress Yarrow's lips. There were smiles from the other women, too, gentle smiles without mockery. "Anything."

"Did your mother not teach you to knit, Mistress Reed?" Miss Malantha asked without looking up from her knitting. She was younger than Hyacinth, her black curls in ribbons, white frills on the edge of her dress. An Elder's daughter, though it was not yet decided if she would marry and stay or be sent away.

"She tried. My sisters were accomplished, but I found my hands more suited for a knife through the deer flesh my father brought home."

Miss Malantha nodded. "We've a shortage of women wishing to butcher the meat."

"That's a Woodsman's wife's job, dear girl," Mistress Yarrow cut in, jabbing a needle in the air as she spoke. "A Boatsman. Your place is here, Mistress Reed, with the..."

"Better folk?" Hyacinth finished, shaking the wool from her fingers.

"Your choice of words, Mistress Reed, not mine."

"You can fetch the old nets from Mr. Carroway, Mistress Reed," Miss Malantha cut in. "They're in need of mending."

Hyacinth nodded, grateful to be relieved. With the help of Mistress Yarrow, Hyacinth had learned how to bottle up the seawater, learned which water weeds were the best to use, and what wax to seal the bottles with. She had gutted and carved the fish bones for the Boatmen each morning and helped sew scraps of fabric for the villagers, her hands growing hard and calloused with the work. She'd been a firm hand on her shoulder, all golden hair and soft eyes, youthful and wise all at once. Hyacinth wanted to resent her, to pull away, but the damned woman would not allow it.

She had stopped dreaming of Abelia and the songs of the trees.

With an awkward goodbye on her lips, Hyacinth left the knitting circle, placing her needles and wool back into the basket. Mistress Yarrow kept her head down, the words between them sour.

Faolan followed behind her as she walked the narrow pathway to the edge of the cliff. From where she stood, skirts billowing, she could just make out the boats as the sea hurled itself forward, tossing them back and forth. She imagined the Boatsmen throwing the sliced and gutted fish back into the Deep, surrounded by the screech of hungry gulls.

Morgan Carroway's cottage looked near to falling from the cliff, its roof tilted, its thatch slick with slimy green. Tools hung from the porch, curved blades, and jagged hooks. His lantern's glass had long been smashed, the fragments lying abandoned within the frame.

"Mr. Carroway?" Hyacinth called, rapping her knuckles on the door. "I've come for the nets that need repairing."

When there came no answer, she pushed open the door and

poked her head into the waiting darkness. With the weak sunlight pushing past the grime on the windows, she made out the remains of a meal on the table, a cup of tea still steaming.

"Hello?" Hyacinth took another step, noticing a door at the back of the cottage, slightly ajar, leading into darkness. "Is anyone there?"

She inched toward the gloom, peering down. Then she heard it. An almost whimper, a soft moaning. Hyacinth plucked a small lantern from the table, lighting it quickly before slipping further into the dark. She set a tentative foot onto the first step leading down to the cellar, hand fumbling over the handrail. Thick webbing broke across her fingers, the scuttle of legs forcing her hand back.

"Miss Lark?" The voice was faint, scratching at the dark. "Is that you?"

Hyacinth held the lantern higher. "No, it's Hyacinth... I've come for the nets, Mr. Carroway. Is all well?"

There was silence for a moment, then a whisper. "No, not really."

Hyacinth strained to see through the gloom. Slowly, she made her way down the old steps, fingers tangling with more cobwebs. The light settled, and she recoiled. Then, she quickly snapped into action.

"Don't move!" She bound down the last of the steps, crouching low to look closer at the man sprawled at the bottom.

Old shelving had fallen across his legs, littering the floor with smashed glass. The shards glinted in the low light, beads of blood shimmering black. But it was his hand that caught Hyacinth's attention, pinned to the floor by one large rusty nail.

"Should have had your sense and lit a lantern," Mr. Carroway murmured.

"Wait, no—"

The echo of her shout was still ringing around the cellar when he forced his hand free, the skin ripping against the reddish nail.

"Oh..." His voice trailed off, faint and shuddering. Mr. Carroway held up his hand, blood spilling from the hole in his hand, down his wrist, his arm, and onto the floor.

"Why? Why would you do that?" Hyacinth fumbled around to find something to stem the bleeding and, finding nothing of use, kicked off her boots and pulled off her stockings.

"Are those clean?"

"Cleaner than a damned rusty nail," she snapped, kneeling so she could wrap his wound. "Are those shelves heavy?"

"Not really... The nail made it a little difficult to get up."

Hyacinth carefully pulled the shelving off him, checking in the low light that no other limb was pinned to the floor. Cuts criss-crossed his arms, flecks of glass glinting against his skin.

"How long have you been down here?" she asked, offering her hand to him. His cold fingers wrapped around hers, his skin ashen.

"A fair while, I would guess." He grunted as she helped haul him to his feet. He wobbled slightly but remained upright.

"I can take a look at your wound upstairs," Hyacinth offered, and he quirked an eyebrow, the lantern light falling softly over his features. "If you would let me, Mr. Carroway?"

"Are you a healer, Mistress Reed?"

She sucked in a breath. "I've cared for enough scrapes and mishaps."

"Your husband does not seem the careless type."

"No, he does not." Hyacinth scooped up the lantern and pointed it towards the stairs. "Are you able to walk?"

"Well enough."

Morgan Carroway followed behind her as she climbed back up the steps, his good hand skimming along the wall, the other held close to his chest. Hyacinth felt his wheezing breath on the back of her neck and hoped the man would not faint. They left the dim cellar together, and she settled the lantern on the kitchen table beside the uneaten food and cold tea.

"I still need the nets," she said, taking in the neglected space around her. The cottage stood in worse repair than hers, the beams overhead cracked and crumbling, the fabric around the grimy windows in tatters, the scraps wavering as the wind blew in. The yellow bones hung above the door needed recarving. "You can keep the stockings."

Morgan Carroway settled himself into a ripped-up armchair with a groan, tilting his head back to rest against the cushion. "They're around back if you think you can manage them on your own."

"I have little choice in that matter, Mr. Carroway." She nodded to his hand, still bound in her good stockings. "Shall we wash that now and rebind it? Else it will go foul, and they'll take your ruined flesh and feed it to the trees."

"Oh, I have no doubts they would."

Hyacinth found a small box of clean linen and salve in the cupboard. The hinges were rusted, the clasp brittle, but there were carvings down the slides, little fishes entwined with reeds, the wings of a sea bird. Pieces of fragmented pearl lay studded in the wood, cloudy and old. She noted Morgan bore more than a few scars on his arms and hands, shining pale against his tanned skin. Everything in the box looked unused, the wax seal on the salve unbroken.

"You do know this will ease any scarring, don't you, Mr. Carroway?" Hyacinth said, holding up the box. "It's not just a pretty treasure."

"I half forgot it was there," he replied with a frown, the subtle lines around his eyes crinkling. "It's not mine, you see, but I doubt the owner would mind me using it."

There was a thickness to his voice, one that stopped Hyacinth from pressing further. He looked at the box as though it were a ghost.

"We wouldn't want that hand to fall off, would we?" Hyacinth attempted to coax a smile from him, taking a moment to follow the sharp line of his cheekbone, the fullness of his lips. His eyes met hers, and she realized she was staring. With a cough, she slipped to her knees with the box and began to clean and dress his hand.

"They fed Wren Jenny's foot to the Teeth," Morgan began, watching Hyacinth work, leaning close. His hand was calloused and stained with blood. He winced as she applied the thick salve to the ragged pieces of skin. "She caught it on a root running from the shadows and snapped her ankle clean. They took it and hung it from the branches, and she swore to me she could hear the trees call her name every night until her wedding eve." He tilted his head back, and Hyacinth noted a sheen of sweat over his brow. "If they called her thereafter, I do not know."

Hyacinth tied off the clean bandage, wiping the blood on her own hands over her skirt. "Do you need a cold cloth for your head, Mr. Carroway? I would rather you did not faint on me."

He laughed then, a quick, low sound. She very much liked the sound of his laugh. "I'll not swoon at your feet, Mistress Reed, don't fret about that."

She chuckled, the small sound settling around the crooked space. "Goodbye, Mr. Carroway."

"Thank you, Hyacinth."

She did not turn at the sound of her name, but it drifted against her all the same, that little piece of her. She left the cottage with blood-splattered arms and cold legs, finding the tangle of broken nets around the back of the cottage.

Afternoon sunshine pierced through the low clouds before Hyacinth finished untangling the nets, her fingers sore from retying the frayed knots and plucking out the remains of old fish from the rope. She preferred it to knitting, her calloused hands more used to rough labor. There was a familiarity to it, not unlike sharpening the tools for the Woodsman, oiling the axes, or rendering fat for the candles. There was little delicacy to Hyacinth, her mother often pointed out; she was hard edges and sharp tongue. Not easy to love.

"I have arranged the thatch to be mended," Sorrell said in greeting, gaze falling on her bare legs and the blood. "You walked across the village like that?"

"I could scarcely fly, my dear." She flicked her boots off, pointing for Faolan to lie down by the fire. "The villagers talk enough as it is."

Sorrell did not bite, and Hyacinth swallowed her disappointment.

"Whose blood?" he demanded.

"Would you care if it was mine?"

"Is it?"

She paused, waiting to read the expression on his face. He remained stoic, eyes soft. "No."

"I went down to the shore with the Elders this morning," he said. "I watched the Boatmen set out, pushing their oars against the waves until they were but tiny dots on the horizon. There is a different sense of fear here, to be surrounded by the trees and the Deep. A tiny island of sanctuary in the middle of such horrors. Can you feel it growing near?" The grin on his face unnerved her, his glee unrestrained, eyes bright. "The damp and the rot? They wish to take it back."

"Whose bones will you use to keep them sated?" The words shook, and she hated that they did. That he could sense her fear.

He stepped close, one finger hooking beneath her chin, forcing it up. "I could hardly send my wife now, could I? Not when she has tried so very hard to make friends here, to settle with the ways of this village. But, if you insist on walking the pathways with your bare legs bloodied..."

"I was assisting an injured man—"

"Without your stockings?" He gripped her chin. "If I cannot feed you to the Teeth, witch, I will see you hanged as a whore."

She smiled back, wide and bared. "And live out your days as a wronged man, guiltless."

"Tread carefully, my dear."

Hyacinth wrenched her face from his hands, offering him no

more harsh woods, only heated silence. She lifted her skirts as she settled beside her dog on the sofa, stretching them out to catch the warmth of the flames. She was not an easy thing to love, but she would not carve herself into likable pieces. Even if she wanted to, she did not know how.

CHAPTER FIFTEEN

yacinth had attended many village dances and festivals, weddings, and name days and feasts to celebrate a good year. She owned one good dress made by her mother from scraps of her wedding gown. It was a simple thing, high-necked and too long, the lace trim always itching against her skin. Her sisters owned similar dresses, all patchworked from pieces of their mother's clothing. Hyacinth could only recall one Elder feast, though the names were long forgotten and the reasons unknown. What she remembered, however, was that, unlike the other celebrations, an Elder feast took place beneath the trees.

A cloudless sky hung overhead, the moon fat. Stars littered the night, some racing across the darkness to places unknown. Hyacinth watched as they shot through the pitch, over the rolling waves and beyond. She felt small, a tiny thing of heartbeats and breath, skin and bone, and little more.

The trees sat quiet, torches casting flickering light over the leaf-strewn ground. The woods were alight with the orange glow, the soil beneath scattered with bone dust. Woodsman stood amongst the trees, masked and silent, watching. They each held their ax, the blades clean and ready.

"Isn't it thrilling," Mistress Yarrow said, hands clutching Hyacinth's arm. "To be so close to the Teeth, to feel the protection granted to us from the Elders."

"I think it is the work of the Woodsman keeping us safe." She pulled her arm away, taking a glass of wine from the table.

"They do fine work." Mistress Yarrow plucked up her own glass and clinked it against Hyacinth's. "To your good health, Mistress Reed, and that of your husband. I pray we always remain good friends."

Hyacinth missed the trust between her sisters, the way they spilled secrets, the way they had curled up together when the storms came—the whispered comfort. The hissed words, the bickering, and the forgiveness. She missed Abelia's raw honesty and the weight of their shared dreams. The way her laugh was just as wicked as her own. Her name on Abelia's lips had always fallen with a grin, a shared knowing. She would never hear her name spoken as such again.

Mistress Yarrow offered a friendship completely unknown to Hyacinth. She knew she could not bear her soul to her and her listen without screaming for the noose. But she had no one else.

"I hope to be very happy here, Mistress Yarrow." The lie fell between them, slipping into the foundations of their companionship. Whether it would solidify or weigh it down, Hyacinth did not know.

Music swelled up from the shadows, played on strings and drums. The sound drifted around Hyacinth, teasing at her feet with the longing to dance. The other village women were already spinning, skirts clutched in their hands, fingers entwined with friends, husbands, and neighbors. There was delight and a sense of freedom in the movement, in the way they laughed, in the way their heads were thrown back as though the Teeth did not matter. Perhaps for that night, they did not.

Mistress Yarrow grasped her hands, pulling Hyacinth into the center of the dance, holding her tight so they spun and spun and spun. Hyacinth kept her eyes open, watching the woods blur by in a mix of firelight and still masks. Hands passed over her, kisses at her cheek, embraces by the women she skinned fish with. There were smiles, and they looked real enough.

"A dance, Mistress Reed?" Elder Yarrow cut in, taking Hyacinth's hands without waiting for an answer. Beside him, Mistress Yarrow seemed to shrink into herself. She cowed before her husband, and Hyacinth disliked the man all the more because of it. He curled one of his around her fingers, lending one too low on her waist. "You have settled well, I hope?"

"Well enough." She smelled brandy on his breath and saw it stained on his lips.

"My wife has long hoped for a good friend, Mistress Reed." He stepped on her toes, his boots scraping over her best shoes. "And I think you are good."

"I do try." She shifted, trying to force space between them.

"I am always here, though," he whispered, words thick. "To listen to any sins before they fester, my dear. I would like to listen to your sins."

"I will keep that in mind."

"I imagine they would taste divine, those sins of yours."

She recoiled, ready to haul her hand back, but someone slammed into Elder Yarrow. He tumbled to the ground, tangling around Morgan Carroway.

"My apologies!" Morgan slurred, attempting to stand and pull the flustered Elder to his feet. He fell against him instead, forcing the other man deeper into the dirt.

"Can I have some assistance!" The Elder's shout caught the attention of the surrounding dancers, and with more than a few titters, Morgan was pulled to his feet.

"The trees above, man!" Elder Yarrow began, dusting off his clothes. "Have you no shame?"

"Not last I checked." Morgan staggered, face streaked with dirt. Someone clapped him on the back, and he grinned. "Fine party, Elder Reed!"

Sorrell stepped beside Hyacinth, wine glass in hand. She fought not to flinch as he placed a hand on her shoulder. "No harm done from what I see, Elder Yarrow. Go sober up, Mr. Carroway, before you truly embarrass yourself." He glanced toward Hyacinth, fingers featherlight on her skin. "All well, dear?"

She met his gaze; his eyes were dark, and his lips reddened. "Quite well, thank you."

"Goodness, darling!" Mistress Yarrow pushed past the growing crowd. "Your robes are ruined. Go change at once." She turned to Hyacinth. "I leave you for one moment and look." She gestured with a smile. "Come dance with us, Mistress Reed."

Hyacinth allowed herself to be dragged from the blustering Elder Yarrow and the cool detachment of her own husband. She brushed against Morgan as she followed her friend, and his words ghosted against her ear, steady and sure.

"You're welcome, Hyacinth."

The night bled on, wine flowing, music pulsing, seeping into the surrounding dark. The Woodsmen remained at the edges, unmoving, moonlight glinting off the blades in their hands.

Hyacinth had lost Sorrell to the dance, and she watched from one of the long tables as he charmed those around him with his lovely smile. Elder Yarrow had not returned, and Hyacinth hoped he was sulking somewhere or fallen into another bottle of brandy. She sipped her wine, swirling the ink-dark liquid in her glass, the taste of elderberries tart on her tongue. Blisters swelled against her feet, red and angry, and she longed to take off her shoes, to feel the cool grass beneath her soles.

From where she sat, she could see Morgan Carroway standing tall and steady, his gaze resting on the dancers. The firelight cast its shadows over the harshness of his face, catching the deep bronze of his hair, the wildness of it. Of him.

He caught her looking with a slow turn of his head, and pushing against the tree he leaned on, he strode toward her. "A dance, Mistress Reed?"

"And have the village tongues wagging?"

"They already do."

She lost sight of Sorrell. No one else had asked her to dance. Morgan Carroway pulled her to her feet, and she winced as her blisters scraped on the leather of her shoes. The music was slowing, more notes falling flat as the wine flowed freely.

His hand was rough in hers; his injured one, still wrapped in gauze, rested high on her waist. They kept the space between them respectable, their arms stretched, no closeness where closeness was not allowed.

"I always found it a little sacrilegious to dance beneath the trees," Morgan said, lightly spinning Hyacinth away before pulling her back. His words were low, for her alone. "It feels as though we taunt the Teeth."

"It shows we are more than our fear of them," Hyacinth countered, eyes fixed on the surrounding dark. Nothing moved, nothing watched back. The Woodsmen stood unflinching, their backs to the dark. The bones in the branches above clicked, keeping time with the beat of the music.

"And what are you made of, Hyacinth?"

"I have yet to find out."

She danced until her feet could take no more, the dull ache sharpening. A few of the villagers had already made for home, Mistress Yarrow included. Sorrell remained, standing at a table beside the other Elders. They watched her, whispering. Elder Lichen lifted a glass in her direction, a smile spreading over his thin face.

"To your good health, Mistress," he called. "May the Oaks bless you."

He made it sound like a warning, and she tried to smile back, keeping her head high. Something pricked against her spine, a growing dread. With a murmured excuse, she made her way back to her cottage, feeling the weight of eyes watching her from the dark.

They came in the night. With silence slipping over the village, wine-soaked and weary, they stepped from the shadows, from the trees.

Hyacinth awoke with the weight of Faolan upon her, his hackles up and lips curled back against his black gums. He uttered a long, low growl, and it thrummed against her cheek. She heard the scraping beyond her window, the click of bone and teeth, the ungodly rattle of something famished.

"They have come!" Sorrell nearly tumbled down the stairs, lantern aloft. "Oaks show us mercy!"

"Put that light out, you damned fool!" Hyacinth hissed, lunging across the floor to snatch it from his hands. The cottage was plunged into total darkness, and gripping both her husband and her dog, she scurried to the wall. The dark was absolute, so heavy it felt almost solid. Hyacinth felt it pressing against her chest, its cold fingers branching out across the floor until not a flicker of light remained.

Sorrell's heart was a drum beside her, his breath almost panting, hot and sweet on her cheek. Faolan stood rigid, his throat rumbling, teeth bared close to Hyacinth's hand.

"Send the dog out—let that devil chase it away." Sorrell's words shook, the breaths between them sharp and quick.

"As an Elder, I believe you should go," she whispered back, not expecting him to move an inch. She was unsure he could, even if he wanted to.

Another rattle silenced them both. They listened as the ground carved open outside their window, a long scrape of taloned bone through dry earth. There came another and another, the clicking of bone and teeth interrupting the stilted quiet. Dampness spread out beside her, and she shifted away, dragging her skirts from the puddle of urine. She held her tongue, granting him a dignity she knew would have never been bestowed upon her.

Hyacinth closed her eyes, squeezing them shut like her father once told her. She wanted to reach for his hand, have his rough voice wash over her. Her fingers raked over the floor instead, fingernails catching in the grain. One tore, ripping clean with a quick slice of pain, and she bit her lip to stop from crying out. She yearned then for any sort of comfort, very nearly reaching out to her husband. Instead, with blood slipping over her fingers, she reached into her pocket, finding her father's fingerbone, and held it tight.

The sound outside was familiar, the sound of bones grating over bone, of claws splintering hard soil. There was the rattle, a low, awful rumbling. It was the sound that had stolen Abelia and devoured her bones. And it was coming for her.

She loathed to cower in the darkness, her heart frantic, bile in her throat. Her spine ached from crouching. She imagined her flesh peeled back by ancient teeth, the slowness of it. Hyacinth clutched the fingerbone tighter, the tip digging deep into her palm. Outside, the world shuddered, the house shook, her bones rattled.

Then a scream came, one far from their little cottage. It tore through the sudden quiet, shattering it completely, wholly. And then it stopped, cut off without an echo as if it had never been.

The Teeth had been sated.

.

CHAPTER SIXTEEN

They remained huddled in the darkness, barely touching, barely breathing. Faolan kept up a constant stream of growls, his huge body quaking against Hyacinth. The village was silent, and only when the watery dawn slipped through the shadows did they dare to stir.

"You'll want to change your robes," Hyacinth said, stretching her cramped limbs. Her hand hovered over the door handle, her breath tight. "Not once can I remember the Teeth coming so close, not into the village proper."

"It can taste the sin here," Sorrell answered, and while his words were heavy with implication, his voice was small. He didn't look at her, did not lay the blame on her wickedness. "The temptation of flesh..." he trailed off, turning to slip back up the stairs.

Hyacinth walked out onto the dew-soaked grass, her good hand tight on Faolan's neck. She had quickly bound her finger, the nail bed throbbing with pain beneath a strip of linen. The dog stood close to her side, his body stiff, lips pulled back. With care, she stepped over the gouged earth, the torn beams, the jagged pieces of stone. Blood spilled down the ruins, blackened and wet, creating trails in the grass that led back into the woods. Hyacinth followed the line of red to where the other villagers gathered. She tried not to look, but look, she did.

The Teeth had taken only a part of Melantha, cleaving her in two. Her torso remained, twisted against hewn earth; the rest was gone.

"The Woodsmen never came home." Mistress Yarrow grasped at Hyacinth's elbow, hands shaking. "No one has seen them."

"Then we need to search the woods—"

"We need to *pray*, Mistress Reed! Gather our senses and meet with the Elders."

"Prayers are little good now. We did pray, we hung the bone, and we carved the wood, and yet they still came." Hyacinth could not tear her eyes away from the twisted body near her feet.

The cage of Melantha's ribs lay open, flayed wide, tendrils of soft, pale skin wavering like bunting. Her eyes were gone, the sockets gaping, already filled with moss.

"Do not let her mother see her like this," Hyacinth said. "We must go into the woods—we need to bring those men home."

Mistress Yarrow's hands trembled, her fingers twisting in the fabric of Hyacinth's sleeve. Others looked on, their clothing speckled with Melantha's blood. Mistress Roan knelt at her head, hands gently stroking back the tangled hair, the dirt, the bloodied earth caked over her skin. Her mouth lay twisted, her jaw clinging by a thread of vine. Hyacinth could see it stretch out over her exposed bones, tethering her to the earth. The air around them hung heavy with shock and fear; a stillness settled as though time itself had paused to wait.

"I said we cavort with trouble beneath those trees," Morgan hissed, stepping up beside Hyacinth so quietly that a jolt went through her. "They didn't even eat her."

"You danced too," she spat back, keeping her voice low. "If you've come here to toss blame about, go elsewhere. Say something cruel in the earshot of grieving folk, and I'll smack you so hard you'll swallow your tongue. Do you understand me, Mr. Carroway?"

"You'd be better off biting off your own."

"Mrs. Fern." Hyacinth ignored him, turning to one of the older women. Her hands were bloodied, her skirts too. She had been kind to Hyacinth, an easy smile never far from her lips. "Your husband is a Woodsman, yes? We need to find them."

"My son, too." Mrs. Fern gripped the wooden token at her neck. "For so long, they kept us safe. I will go with you."

"And I will."

"For my brother, I will go too."

"Let us bring them home."

There was a quiet chorus of voices, small offerings to tread into the dark, without mask or bone to bring those lost back home. It stirred something in Hyacinth, tampering down the fear, the loss until it became something else entirely.

Morgan stepped forward, eyes lingering on the torn remains of Melantha. He bent low, kneeling on the blood-dampened ground to pull at the greenery threading through her remains. "Someone fetch a blanket, anything to put her in. Else, she'll be knotted to the earth."

Hyacinth joined him, ripping the roots left behind by the Teeth, wrenching them from the exposed pieces of pelvis. She carefully folded skin and bone into a rough, woven bed sheet. It was an unfitting funeral shroud, but at least there were pieces to bury. It was more than Abelia had.

"Are you ready to wander into the woods?" Morgan wiped the blood from his hands on his trousers.

"Will you be joining us, Mr. Carroway?"

"Aye, Mistress. Couldn't well leave you to wander the woods."

More voices joined, words shaking, whispered, fear-soaked. But they rose in a collective echo. The Elder Wives remained silent. Mistress Roan would not meet Hyacinth's eye; instead, she kept her attention on the bloodied bedsheet, with prayers quick on her lips.

"We will gather at the Drove," Mistress Yarrow began, her fingers digging sharply into Hyacinth's shoulder. "There will be no more talk of going into the woods. The Elders will know what needs to be done."

"The Elders hide away while good men are lost," Hyacinth snapped. "Go say your prayers, Mistress Yarrow. They're of no use here."

Hurt flashed across Mistress Yarrow's face. "It is heresy to go into those woods."

"Cowardice is heresy, Mistress Yarrow," Morgan said. "Or so I was told, I bear the scars from it. I would rather bleed for the Teeth than from the hands of your husband again."

Hyacinth waited a beat, but no more arguments came. Her decisions had been made—she would lead the others into the woods, and damned be the consequences. She thought about her own father, how he wandered, without fear or complaint, into the darkness. If he had not come home, if she knew he remained beneath the boughs, lost with the Teeth, there would be no force strong enough to stop her from going in after him. These men were fathers, sons, husbands, friends. Pretty words were no help, and Hyacinth refused to waste her breath on them.

The tables and chairs, lanterns, glasses, and plates had been cleared away from the woods from the night before, the ground raked clean as though no one had been there at all. Not a trace of the festivities remained, as was the custom.

It was a foolish thing to dance beneath the oaks, even close to the edge as they had been. But it was how things were done: to welcome in a new Elder, to show the Teeth that the rules were followed, the bones carved, and the words spoken. It was a show of devotion, not a taunt.

Or so she had been told.

Though she would not speak it, Hyacinth agreed with Morgan.

She followed closely behind him, the winding path beneath her feet clear, stripped back as it should be. Morning sunlight shone down through the branches above, catching the golden-touched leaves before they started to fall. A faint chill carried on the wind, bringing with it the scent of moss and decay, a foreboding promise of winter hardship. The branches creaked, the ropes of teeth clicking gently together.

"How far are we to go in, Mr. Carroway?" Hyacinth asked, straining to hear the sounds of the woods, the call of heathens. But there was no singing, no wildling laughter. No birdsong either, just the creak of the branches and the rattle of bones.

"I fear if we carry on this path and still find no trace, we'll likely not find anything whole."

No counter was made. To come this far into the woods, away from the village, was madness; Hyacinth knew that, and to bring others with her was near unforgivable. The village women looked to her, their faces a mix of terror and hope.

They made no sounds on the forest path, their boots creeping with care over the bare earth. The trees around them were still, the shadows, too. Hyacinth could feel it deep within her, the knowing of being watched.

Shadows stretched out over the ground, weaving over the roots and vines. The path grew wilder, the edges growing over, the forest taking it back piece by piece. And still, they walked on. In the branches above, the knotted bones grew older, in dire need of being replaced. They were yellow things, moss-coated and brittle.

Thoughts of Abelia drifted over Hyacinth, the way she had danced and slipped into darkness. Hyacinth was traveling further than she had that night, following the winding paths to the very edges of where the Woodsmen worked. She stared through the wild, straining her eyes wide. She longed for one glimpse of her, one memory whole and hers. What did it matter that she was too far from the picked bones of Abelia to find her?

"Wait." Morgan thrust his arm out, pressing his hand against the center of her chest to stop her. "Don't...don't look."

He had stopped where the trees stood knotted, branches interwoven so tightly that scarcely any light could bleed through. Her heartbeat thumped against his hand, and he pulled away.

"I need to see," she replied, glancing back at the other women, those she had led into the woods. "As the wife of an Elder, it is my duty to bear the burden of the Teeth."

"You don't half-talk some bullshit," Morgan hissed, low enough for only her ears to hear. His face was bloodless, his lips too.

Hyacinth braced herself as the other women stayed back, unwilling to see the horrors for themselves. Then she stepped past Morgan, and this time, his hand went to her shoulder, not to pull her away, but to rest there, an assurance that she was not alone. Her breath caught in her throat, curdling against her tongue until it fell as a garbled cry past her lips.

They stood in a perfect circle, the Woodsmen, standing tall and silent as they had the night of the dance. Branches of oak and elm sprouted from their gaping mouths, their jaws hanging loose, knotted with vines. It trailed over their arms, tangling at their feet to hold them to the earth, moss and lichen clinging to their torn, ashen skin. From eyeless sockets, brown fungi grew, dripping down cleaved bone to take root and spread elsewhere.

"Merciful Oaks." Hyacinth stumbled back, bile burning in her throat. "We can't leave them there!"

"They are a warning, Hyacinth." Morgan clutched at her wrist, pulling her sharply away. "They came into the village last night, taking only one girl, then claimed our Woodsmen as their own. They are angry."

"I can see that." She pulled free of his grasp, turning her back on the rooted Woodsmen. "So, who in this damned village has pissed them off?" She shivered, acid burning in her throat. From where she stood, she could hear *them,* a gentle rattle, soft hisses slipping through the boughs.

"Go, go back," she breathed, nearly pushing Mrs. Fern. "We must go back."

"They're... Are they gone?"

Hyacinth nodded, though the simple word could not begin to convey what had happened to those poor men. Gone...like Abelia had gone, like Melantha, like the poor girl whose name she never learned that was snatched by the Deep. Gone was too gentle a word, too soft. A lie. But it was also a small comfort, and it was all Hyacinth could offer the women.

"Yes."

"Is there anything left..."

"Go home, Mrs. Fern." Hyacinth steeled her voice, mimicking the way she had heard the other Elder Wives speak. "Join the others in their prayers. It is not safe to linger here."

It was as though she had conjured it, the sudden darkening of the skies, the gathering of clouds. The scant light from before winked out, and a blanket of nothingness swept over them all. Thunder rolled, and a scream pierced Hyacinth's ear, her own dangling from her tongue.

"Make haste," Hyacinth hissed, clutching Mrs. Fern's hand. "Hold onto one another, and do not let go."

Hyacinth felt the roughness of Morgan's hand snatch at hers, and she allowed him to lead them through the pitch.

Branches snapped underfoot, the air around them shuddering with thunder. Lightning flashed, a sharp burst of white, and Hyacinth saw Them. A second, no more, and They were gone. But They watched. From beyond the boughs, taller than the trees, They stood. They watched. Giant, inhuman things with no discernable features, yet They watched.

Hyacinth was certain no one else saw them, for no one paused; only she faltered, almost tripping. Morgan glanced back, his hold on her tightening. "Stop looking into the shadows." His voice was low, meant for her alone.

She heeded his advice, focusing on his dark shape before her. Morgan carried on leading them through the woods, his pace quick, almost frantic. Hyacinth could feel his hand tremble, feel the slick-ness of it, mingling with hers. After what seemed like an eternity, she felt their terrible presence lift.

"They were so close," she whispered to Morgan. "They could have reached out and plucked us from the earth."

"It is a mercy they spared us."

"Is it a mercy, do you think? Truly?"

"It matters little what I think, Hyacinth."

The trees thinned, the bones tied swinging with the growing

wind. There was a cold dampness to the air, a heaviness to the bruise-like clouds. The gulls swooping close to the cliff screeched, and the skies screamed back. Rain came in sheets, soaking them all quickly to the bone. Hyacinth paused at the edge of the village, her back to the woods, allowing the white-faced, silent women to walk ahead.

Morgan fell back and kept pace beside her. His stride matched hers; he was too close. She could hear his breaths, the ragged inhale, the shudder of it passing his lips. He made to catch her arm again, and she smacked him away.

"You will lose a finger if you keep doing that, Morgan Carroway."

"You are new to this village," he began, holding both hands up. "The Teeth have stayed away for some time now, and they are not just hungry. They are angry."

Something twisted in her stomach, something dreadful. She met his eyes. "I am often blamed for things not of my doing. Do you think I called down the Teeth?"

"No."

The single word was a solid thing, too small, she thought, to carry with it such meaning.

"But the village will, Hyacinth."

She sighed, resigned. "As long as they have someone to burn, to hang, to pluck the bones from, who really minds if they carry the sins or not."

"I care."

She held his gaze. "You shouldn't."

Hyacinth stood before the dais in the Drove, flanked by the women who had braved the woods with her. She stared up at the seated men, past their masks to the cowards beneath.

Elder Yarrow was the first to speak, voice ringing out over the silent Form. "You disobeyed our Word and went into the shadows, did you not, Mistress Reed?"

She did not need to look at her husband to feel the weight of his gaze upon her, the fury burning in his eyes. She wondered if he was afraid...not for her, but for his own neck.

"I did." She kept her back straight. "I urged the others to follow me. Any heresy here is mine alone."

"And Mr. Carroway?"

"He tried to force me back..."

"I did no such thing, Elder Yarrow!" Morgan cut in, throwing Hyacinth a look of utter rage. "We went to bring those men home, knowing the prayers here were not listened to, not heeded, not wanted."

"You dare—"

"We dared, Elder Sir!"

"Are you to hang the bloody lot of us?" Hyacinth demanded, gesturing to the tear-stained women, their faces like ghosts. They looked as though they would not fight the noose or the flames.

"Be calm!" Elder Lichen called out, rising beside Elder Yarrow. His thin fingers steepled before him as he looked over the crowd. "You will not hang, Mistress Reed, not tonight, for I have it on record you were granted permission to slip into the woods. Is that not correct, Mistress Yarrow?" His smile was an odd thing, showing too many teeth, revealing too much glee for such a terrible situation.

Mistress Yarrow stood, her shaking hands rubbing the wrinkles from her apron. She had brushed her hair, the gold strands smooth and shiny, pinned beneath a pretty headscarf. She looked almost unruffled if not for her trembling fingers. "Mistress Reed obtained word from my husband, Elder Sir. I overheard it before I went to say my own prayers. For all the good they do."

"That is a damned lie!" Elder Yarrow bellowed. The whiskers on his mask quivered, making him look even more ridiculous.

Hyacinth swallowed her laugh before she choked on it.

"Perhaps you lost your memory in that bottle of brandy, dear,"

Mistress Yarrow whispered, loud enough for only the Elders and Hyacinth to hear.

There was a pause, and all masked faces turned toward Elder Yarrow.

"My wife committed no sins in going into the woods," Sorrell interrupted, his voice even. "She found the Woodsmen and braved the shadows to seek out their lost souls."

Elder Lichen peered down at Hyacinth as if determining his next move. "There will be no punishment for you, Mistress Reed," Elder Lichen decided. He bent down beside her so the ragged whiskers of his mask pressed against her cheek. "But I cannot bestow a blessing upon you in the wake of such horrors. May you go with Grace."

"At your word," she murmured, fighting the urge to lean away.

"And who are we to feed to the Teeth?" Elder Yarrow hissed. "To quell their growing appetites? To atone for the sins that anger them so?" He raised a finger, pointing to Hyacinth for a breath, one more, and then, "Morgan Carro—"

"Leave the lad be, Elder Yarrow." Mr. Douglas shoved his way to the front of the hall. "You're down six good men, you brainless fool, and you're going to send one strong as he to the Teeth? Send yourself, and let them feast on your hollow skull."

"I will have you hanged!"

"What is the meaning of this, Mr. Douglas?" Elder Roan asked sternly. He looked around at his fellow Elders as though hoping someone would quickly put a stop to the meeting and save them all the embarrassment.

"You need someone for the Teeth? Someone to stuff full of your sins and leave to the shadows? I would reckon my bones would do a fine job."

"Are you quite mad?" Elder Roan asked, fish sales glinting. Oily black leaked from the edges of his mask, slipping down his cheek like tears.

"Aye, likely." Mr. Douglas looked to Hyacinth, giving her a quick nod. "I doubt you'll have any other offers, though."

"You choose this freely?" Sorrell asked. "Knowing what will become of you? There will be nought left, but the stripped bones we will carve..."

He shrugged. "I know the ins of it, boy."

"You do not have to do this," Morgan said. "I am not owed some fickle self-sacrifice."

"You're owed what I say you're owed, lad." Mr. Douglas stretched his hands out to the Elders, his head back, a strange grin on his wrinkled face. "Take me to the Teeth, gentlemen."

"No!" Morgan stormed forward, boots echoing. "Don't you fucking dare!"

"Sit down!" Elder Yarrow bellowed. "Be thankful, Mr. Carroway. Not all cowards are granted such a boon."

Morgan lunged, scrabbling against the dais to haul Elder Yarrow to the floor. They fell in a heap of fists and rage to the startled gasps of those gathered and to the cold bemusement of the watching Elders.

They hesitated, the Elders; Hyacinth could sense it. The sound of Morgan's fists landing on the soft flesh of Elder Yarrow echoed around the Drove, unrelenting, and it was not before Elder Lichen raised his thin, crooked hand did they stop. Morgan was hauled away by four Boatman, his knuckles bloodied, his face twisted with rage and despair. Hyacinth stepped forward, and he looked at her, eyes shining. Then they went wide, the sharp echo of wood against bone shuddering against the quiet. He fell, blood at his temple, beneath his fingernails, and did not move.

CHAPTER SEVENTEEN

"Come, Mistress Reed."

A hand gripped Hyacinth's elbow, forcing her away from the dais, from the Elders, from Morgan sprawled out over the flagstones. But before she could gently remove Mistress Yarrow's hand, Sorrell joined them, his hand landing forcefully at her shoulder. She was being herded, and she cared little for it.

"I am not some weak-minded girl," she hissed, planting her feet.

Mistress Yarrow did not release her hold, but her husband dropped his hand.

"I am in no danger of collapse—leave me be."

"How fortunate you are that you can hide behind that impenetrable facade of yours," Sorrell breathed in her ear. "but let something rattle your sensibilities, for mercy's sake!"

"Let's get some tea into you," Mistress Yarrow said. "You're freezing, Mistress Reed. Sorrell, dear, help her inside."

Firm hands steered Hyacinth away so she could not see Mr. Douglas or the other Elders. Where they had led him to, she knew not. Mistress Yarrow guided her back to her own cottage, Sorrell closely following behind them. Hyacinth found herself thankful that she would not have to endure the cold darkness of Mistress Yarrow's dwelling. She fell onto the sofa, pulling Faolan close as he clambered atop her. He smelled of the cottage, of woodsmoke and slightly damp fur, of soil and moss. His coarse coat scratched against her cheek, bringing with it a comforting heat, a closeness she had missed and longed for.

"Do you think he knew?" Hyacinth asked, her arms tight around the neck of her dog. "That he would give himself to the Teeth?"

The sofa dipped beside her, Mistress Yarrow perching on the edge, not touching the great gray beast towering over her. "I am not surprised by his decision."

"Why?"

"He thinks Mr. Carroway's soul is worth more than his own."

Confused, Hyacinth looked up, her head still resting on the solid weight of Faolan. "And is it?"

"You would have to ask him."

"But I am asking you, Mistress Yarrow," Hyacinth said, sensing the other woman's discomfort. "What has Morgan Carroway done to risk the Teeth?"

"He is a coward, wife," Sorrell answered, taking his place in the armchair, away from the two women. "Perhaps you can coax the story from him when you see him next?"

There was a sneer to his voice, an attempt to bait her into an argument; Hyacinth could feel it. She smiled back instead. "Are you granting me leave to go see him then, husband?"

Hyacinth reveled in the way his eyes darkened, how his lips thinned.

"I feel you have taken enough of his time of late."

The air between them thickened, a weight of loathing and spite filling the room as quickly as the woodsmoke from a fire. Beside Hyacinth, Mistress Yarrow tensed, her discomfort obvious.

"You were fortunate, Mistress Reed," she began, "that your husband so bravely stepped in to support you and your decision to go wandering the woods."

Hyacinth bristled. "If you believe he did so out of concern for me, Mistress Yarrow, then you are a damned fool."

"Fool or not, you are sitting here now because of what he did." Mistress Yarrow swiped at her eyes, dashing away the tears forming there. "Goodness, fill your head with some sense before you find a noose tightening below it!"

Hyacinth regretted causing the tears on Mistress Yarrow's pale cheeks, though she could not find it in herself to regret her words. She turned back to her husband, who watched them both with bright eyes. "If I carried the judgment alone, and you could step back and watch me swing without falling from favor, would you still have spoken?"

He shrugged, a lazy gesture, as though her life truly meant nothing. "We will never know, will we, dear wife?"

But she did.

"You call Morgan Carroway a coward, but you hide your cowardice behind that mask of yours. With it, you never have to venture into the Deep or find yourself beneath the trees with the Teeth at your heels," Hyacinth spat out the words, her anger a solid, choking thing.

"Stop, Mistress Reed." Mistress Yarrow placed a firm hand on Hyacinth's shoulder, her fingers digging into the fabric of her sleeve. With a rasping sigh, she stood, making her way over to the stove to make tea. She bashed the kettle down on the burner with more force than necessary. "You are upset, but that does not excuse blasphemy."

"It falls often from her tongue." Sorrell turned to Hyacinth. "Does it not, wife?"

"I believe we just have different words for truth."

He gave no retort but leaned back in his chair, taking the mug of black tea Mistress Yarrow offered him. Hyacinth's cups and saucers were not nearly as fine as Mistress Yarrow's; they were plain and earthen, and the glaze chipped in places. But they were a wedding gift from her mother, a piece of home. Her father's hands had once held them. She would never feel their closeness again, but the echoes of memory would be enough. She admired them now as Mistress Yarrow handed her a cup, letting its warmth soothe her hands.

"There are no cakes, I'm afraid," she said, scalding her lip on the too-hot drink. "I have not had the time to make any. I was not expecting guests."

"I would not expect you to," Mistress Yarrow replied, slipping back beside Hyacinth, hand wrapped around her own cup of tea. "It takes time to find your feet here, my dear. We are friends, and your company is enough."

"Is there anyone looking after Mr. Carroway?" Hyacinth asked into the falling quiet. "A blow to the head like that would knock the senses out of anyone."

They both ignored Sorrell's snort.

"One of the Woodsman's wives will be, I would imagine." Mistress Yarrow placed her empty teacup down. "Mrs. Marmor is usually called upon to tend to the sick."

"He is not sick though, is he?" Hyacinth stood, shaking off the dog hair on her skirts.

"Where do you think you are going?" Sorrell demanded, knuckles white as they gripped his teacup, the liquid inside undrunk. "To him? Are you so ready and willing to be named a whore?"

"For tending to someone in need? To someone who was hurt because of my choices and my actions? Who would think a whore of me for simple kindness, husband, apart from you?" Hyacinth turned to Mistress Yarrow, her gaze scathing. "Are those your thoughts too, Mistress Yarrow?"

"Would it surprise you if I told you no?"

"It would... It does."

There was a sadness to the woman's smile. "It is no sin to look upon one's neighbor, especially when in need," Mistress Yarrow said softly. "Who do we have, if not each other?"

"Then I will go and relieve Mrs. Marmor. I am sure she is a busy woman. I will check on Mr. Carroway and return shortly."

"You have a kind heart," Mistress Yarrow said before Sorrell could breathe another word. "A kind soul, Mistress Reed."

"I have been told otherwise."

"Then they do not see you as I do."

Hyacinth paused, fingers curling around the door handle. She doubted that anything good could be seen, buried deep beneath the wickedness, the too-sharp pieces of her. She had looked at her reflection often enough to know there was no softness behind her eyes, nothing lovely. Whatever Mistress Yarrow thought she saw was hope and fancy, an echo of the sweetness of her own heart.

"Thank you for your quick thinking earlier," she said at last, feeling the strange threads of friendship tighten. The door clicked shut behind her, and Hyacinth waited a moment, listening behind the wood. There came whispers, an easy chatter in her absence, though she could not make out the words.

Faolan followed her across the quiet pathways, the sun already making its descent below the tree line, stretching out the shadows, long-limbed and dark. The lanterns on the porches flickered, guiding lights to an empty watch. Hyacinth looked to the trees, and they stood silent and unmoving. If what lay within lay slumbering, full and satisfied, she did not know.

The door to Morgan's cottage swung open as she approached, hand raised to knock on the cracked wood.

"Blessed Oaks, you startled me, Mistress Reed." A stout older woman stood at the doorway, thick silver hair bundled in a knot at her nape. "Are you here to see the man with more brawn than sense?"

Hyacinth smiled. "I am, Mrs. Marmor."

"Well, that is a blessing. I've got three babes in arms back home, and I can't sit and play nursemaid here." The woman chuckled at Hyacinth's look of shock. "Not my own babies, girl. Mine are long grown, but daughters have their own, and I have arms to spare, wrinkled as they may be."

"Their menfolk..." Hyacinth began, the image of the rooted Woodsmen too clear in her mind. She could still smell the rot, the strange spice of old oaks, of undergrowth and fungi.

"We are a family of Boatmen," Mrs. Marmor said gently. "To the Deep we go, and never have I been so thankful. Those poor souls." The old woman clasped the circlet at her neck, whispering a few words.

Hyacinth remained silent, not joining in with prayers of her own.

"I've left some broth warming on the stove for when he wakes," Mrs. Marmor said, gathering her skirts. "And there's more laudanum on the bedside table."

"For a head wound?"

She was given a shrug as an answer. "Elder Lachlan's orders."

Hyacinth stepped over the threshold of Morgan's cottage, leaving Faolan to sniff around outside, ears up and tail low. She paused to stir the thick soup slowly bubbling on the stove, turning her nose up at the grayish blobs of meat floating to the top.

"Mr. Carroway?" she called up the stairs, hand resting on the banister, the wood splintering against her palms. The carvings in the beams were faded, the overgrown moss thick. The sun-bleached, brittle bones hanging at the windows crumbled as she brushed past them. She thought of her own home, with its deep carvings and white bone, and how none of it had kept her father safe. Or her.

Up she went, steps creaking beneath her feet. She tapped lightly on the door to his bed-chamber, and when no answer came, she slipped in. Candlelight flickered on the crate Morgan used as a bedside table; the fat candle nearly burned down to a stub. A green vial sat beside it, the contents almost gone.

"Are you asleep or dead, Mr. Carroway?"

She leaned over him, but he did not stir. Dried blood caked his left temple, clumping in his bronze hair. Hyacinth pressed two

THE BONE DRENCHED WOODS

fingers to the crook of his neck, feeling the slow thump of his pulse under her fingertips. "You foolish man."

Hyacinth heaved him onto his side, forcing the thin pillows behind his back to stop him from rolling back over. She had done the same for her father at times, with the help of her mother, when he had come stumbling home after a night of hard drinking.

It was not uncommon for Woodsmen to fall into drink, to slip into the small tavern nestled out of sight. It kept them warm, her mother had told her, kept the fear away so they would go back out night after night after night. She often likened the smell of hops to her father coming home, the scent comforting. If he stumbled or walked with his head high, it didn't matter as long as he came home.

Hyacinth lowered herself onto a nearby chair. The heaviness of all that had just transpired weighed down on her, and she suddenly felt quite exhausted. She closed her eyes, head against the wall, lulled by the soft rumbles of Morgan's snores. She was in the woods again, her feet bare, the soil damp and cold. It pricked at her skin, a chill of dying leaves and early frost. She stood alone, waiting.

The music came before Abelia did, a sorrowful call played out over the branches, the tall grass, the decaying leaves. She emerged from the shadows, dancing and twirling on tiptoes, her hands reaching toward the star-swallowed skies.

"Come dance," she sang, holding one flesh stripped hand out. Her fingers dangled, sinew torn loose. From the cracks in her marrow bloomed wide-headed fungus, as gray as the sap slipping over her face, her neck. "Come dance with us, Hyacinth."

Hyacinth took a step, another, feet dragging along the ground. Closer and closer, she walked, her hand reaching out for Abelia, fingers curling around the rot-sodden remains of her friend. "I am afraid..."

The words fell into the wind, snatched away before they were heard.

"I have to go back..."

"To where, Hyacinth?" Abelia sang, lips stretching wide.

"Where will you go where they will not hunger for your bones? Thirst for your sins?"

"Let me go!"

Abelia's mouth yawned open, her eyes white and wide, still leaking that gray sap. They looked like tears, leaving tracks against her skin. "You should have stayed with me. With us."

The grip on Hyacinth's fingers tightened, bone digging into her flesh. With a sharp tug, she was pulled close, a hand at her cheek, almost soft. Lips pressed against hers, gentle and warm, the taste and stench of rot gone.

"Come dance with me..."

A low moan woke her, echoing alongside the sound of a *thump, thump, thump.* With a jolt, she sat up, dashing away the grittiness in her eyes with the back of her hand. She licked her lips, searching for the taste of the woods, of Abelia, and found nothing.

"Get away!"

The words came muffled, nearly swallowed by the hulking great dog at the bedside. Faolan sat, head towering over Morgan, tongue lapping his cheek. His tail whacked the floorboards, sending up clouds of dust with each thump.

"Call off your damned beast, woman!"

Hyacinth hurried to remove her dog, forcing him back down near her feet. He whined, his soulful black eyes pleading up on her, but down he remained.

"How is your head?" she asked Morgan, settling back in her chair.

"Feels like it's been cracked open and scooped out," Morgan replied, scrubbing a hand over his cheek to remove the slobber left behind. "For a moment, I thought it was your vile breath that woke me."

"You are a charming man, Morgan Carroway." Hyacinth stood. "Now that I see you are not dead, I shall take my leave."

He grinned. "How long did you watch me sleep?"

"Long enough to check you were still with us, long enough to roll you on your side so—"

He heaved, vomiting onto the floor.

"...you wouldn't choke when you did that."

He sat up, wiping his mouth. "Have they taken him?"

All traces of humor slipped away, leaving the harsh lines of his jaw to stand out. Hyacinth hovered, wondering if she should leave, clean up the mess he'd made, or sit beside him. Nothing seemed to be the right thing to do, so she remained standing, looking down at him.

"I believe so. They are to give Mr. Douglas to the Teeth tonight."

He made a small noise, not quite a cry, but filled with a heavy sense of sorrow all the same.

Mind made up, Hyacinth sat beside him, reaching across the blankets to take his hand in hers. "Who is he to you?" she asked softly.

He took a moment to answer, head slipping once more against the pillows. "My father, Hyacinth."

Hyacinth met his eyes, the weight of his words pressing against her. She had watched her father die at the hands of the Elders, and Morgan was powerless to save his own. She understood the heavy use of laudanum to keep him quiet—and away.

"I am sorry," she said, wishing she had more to say than empty platitudes. She had never been good at offering comfort, any softness lingering within her long carved out. Her sisters seemed to know when to draw someone close, how to whisper words of hope and dry tears. Her mother, like Hyacinth, did not. Perhaps they were more alike than she had once thought.

"Someone must always be fed to the Teeth," Morgan replied.

"Does it make it easier to know that, then?"

He gave a rough laugh devoid of humor. "You'd have thought we were all used to it by now. Our hearts deadened by relentless loss."

Hyacinth shifted in her chair. She would toss her grief to the Teeth if she could, if they would eat that instead of flesh. She would let it all go, the pain of losing Abelia and her father, and feel nothing at all. Emptiness would be easier.

"Perhaps if the Elders preached only fear and left out any ideas of light and hope, we would be better off. Tell us we're fucked, and leave us be."

Morgan closed his eyes, his hand warm in Hyacinth's. "Then what use would we have for them, Hyacinth?"

She squeezed his fingers before drawing them to her lips, placing the faintest of kisses on his knuckles. "What use indeed?"

"My father and I were never close," Morgan began thickly. "Even as a young boy, he never really liked me, then after..." He trailed off, voice slurring.

"After what?"

Hyacinth had seen the scars on his back, the shining white lashes. She knew he was given a whipping for cowardice, but she did not understand what he had run from. "Morgan?"

"We were not on good terms, my father and I," he said.

"May I ask why?"

"He was a Boatman a long time ago," Morgan replied, his words slipping together. "My mother worked down by the coast preparing the fish for the Deep, weaving the nets with the other women. My sister, too. The work of the Boatmen would have been my calling, predestined whether I wanted to take up the oars or not; it mattered little. We lived on the edge then, teetering close to the cliff edge with a few of the other Boatmen. As close to the Deep as we could be while still on land. We hung the bones, we carved the words, we fed the Deep, and still it came." He stopped to take another drink, another and another until he once again held an empty cup. His words were quick and quiet, and Hyacinth dared not stop him lest a break in the torrent of words choke him into silence.

"The Boatmen were out, casting their nets beneath the moonlight. From my window, I could just make out their lanterns bobbing out on the waves, far out over the Deep. And then the skies grew black, darker than the night, a solid black that made it hard to breathe. We could scarcely see the flames from the candles, the lanterns in the distance all but gone. The waves rose, crashing up against the windows and the side of the cottage, breaking glass. My mother screamed for me, and my sister too, as the water spilled in, rushing through the broken windows. It dragged them away, all white foam and twisted weed. I watched on from the staircase, water at my feet. And I ran. While the Deep took my mother and sister, their screams following behind, I tore upstairs and jumped from my parents' window. My left leg snapped, but while my home was dragged into the waves, I crawled away."

Hyacinth felt her heart twist, aching for the young boy he had once been. She reached out to lay a gentle hand on Morgan's arm. "How old were you?"

He didn't look at her. "Twelve."

Too young to be hanged as a coward, Hyacinth knew. Not young enough to escape a lashing.

"My father heard their screams," Morgan continued, drawing away from Hyacinth's touch. Beside him, Faolan let out a low whine. "The way they called my name, begged for help. Thirteen Boatmen lost their lives that evening. Eight houses pulled into the Deep. Thirty-one souls in all were devoured."

"You could not have saved them."

He was quiet for a long while, head back. For a moment, Hyacinth wondered if he had surrendered to sleep. Then he murmured, "There was time, Hyacinth."

Hyacinth had noticed a stiffness in his walk when she had helped him after his fall, putting it down to bruises from the tumble. She wondered if anyone had helped him, if they had set the break, or left him to put himself back together.

"My father was injured enough that he could no longer work on the boats. He was given a cottage and was looked after by the village. He did not speak to me again."

"Did he witness your punishment?" She could not imagine such a horror; to watch one of her siblings tied and lashed was unthinkable, even Briony.

"He was the one who delivered it." Morgan's head lolled on the pillow, slumber claiming him quickly. His lips parted, a slither of drool slipping from his open mouth.

Hyacinth watched the slow rise and fall of Morgan's chest, the weight of his words pressing against her. With care, she adjusted the pillows behind Morgan's head, then fetched a bucket and soapy water to clean the floor. She took the laudanum, slipping it into her apron pocket.

"Stay, Faolan," she ordered, though the dog had not moved. He watched her before turning his great head and resting it upon the bed. Hyacinth smoothed out her skirts and walked away, pausing to remove Mrs. Mamor's congealing soup from the stove before she left.

CHAPTER EIGHTEEN

T he warmth of Hyacinth's cottage soaked into her bones. A
fire roared over fat logs with hungry flames. If she had not
been so chilled, she would have worried that the thatch
would catch alight.

She already missed Faolan, but she knew he was best at
Morgan's side. She knew too well how painful it was to watch a
parent be put to death. There was a way to do such things, for sacrifices. They were to be respectful and calm, a circle of masks, bone,
and silence save for the rites uttered from holy tongues. But it did
little to alleviate the horror of it all. As the wife of an Elder, she
would be expected to be present for the sacrifice, and she too
would be given a mask. She would watch the Teeth take Mr.
Douglas, and she was to be silent when They did.

"That's the last of the damned wood," Sorrell said from his
crouched position in front of the fire. "Mistress Yarrow offered
some logs from her supply, but I fear she also has few to spare."

With the nights turning colder, it would have been time for the
Woodsmen to go deeper into the trees to cut dry wood for the fires.
There should never be a shortage of firewood, but then, there
should never be a shortage of Woodsmen. It would have been easy

LV. RUSSELL

for Hyacinth to slip near the edges of the wood and collect the fallen boughs, the pieces left to rot into the earth. But to take unblessed wood, to snatch it from the shadows, to steal it away, was unforgivable. If the Teeth did not find her, then the noose surely would.

"Have you chosen the new Woodsmen yet?" Hyacinth remained standing close to the carved bundle of bones beside the doorway.

Sorrell continued to kneel by the fire, wiping pieces of bark and dust from his trousers. "We have, though they will not set foot beneath the boughs until the bones of Mr. Douglas have been stripped and hung."

"Then we will have a few cold nights," she said. Sorrell turned at her tone, eyebrow raised.

"You disapprove."

"Does it matter?"

"No."

He poked at the flames, sending sparks up the chimney. The cottage smelled of smoke and tea, the dampness burned away by smoldering wood. There was a sweetness to it, one that settled over everything, reminiscent of home. If she closed her eyes, Hyacinth could almost imagine herself back in her cottage, the noise of her sisters nearby, the sound of her mother's skinning knife slashing through flesh, the thud of her father's boots on the worn floor. Rarely was there ever silence or the solitude she once longed for. She wanted to go home, although she no longer knew what that meant.

"Do you think..." She stopped, swallowing back the words dangling from her tongue.

"Go on." Sorrell shifted out of his crouched position to sit against the armchair, stretching his legs out before him. He looked odd on the floor, almost relaxed, flames dancing in his eyes, catching the gold in his hair. There was coal dust on his cheek.

She sighed, settling beside him, close but not touching. "Do you really think that this is all there is to life? Staving off an endless hunger?"

His eyes narrowed at her blasphemy, but he did not scold her. Instead, he shrugged. "Maybe once it was something different, or more than this. I know not. If there is an ending, I will not live to see it, nor will you."

It was the most honest answer he had given her, and it lacked bite.

"It rattled you, didn't it?" she said, a nudge to see if he would snap. "When the Teeth came so close by."

He stared back. "Only a fool...or a witch would be unnerved."

"I am no witch."

Sorrell shifted, moving closer to her, his nose near touching hers. There was the scent of mint tea on his breath, a coolness to his words. "And I am no deviant."

"I am not lying. I have never—"

"There are no lies on my tongue either, wife!" he hissed, hand clamping down on hers before she could move away.

"I heard the stories they told about you." Hyacinth twisted her hand, her nails digging into the soft flesh of his palm. "The things you did, the blood you drew, the pain you wrought..."

"From the same mouths that would have you burned, that had Emory Merrow shot, that hanged your father."

"You tightened that noose!"

"Aye, Hyacinth, I did. If not me, then it would have been another. Your father was doomed to die that day, you know that."

"So you're an innocent man!" She laughed in his face.

"I am as innocent as you are, dear wife." He bared his teeth back at her. "So not at all, not in the slightest."

"So why did they shackle you to me? Why get rid of you? What did you do to piss those Elders off?"

Sorrell cupped her chin with his free hand. "I fucked Elder Lachlan's wife on the evening I took my vows. Took Aviana dressed in my robes with a newly skinned mask." He leaned in closer. "I also had a parchment holding twelve signatures to have him struck off for the unspeakable things he did."

"It's true then, the rumors?" Hyacinth asked, a morbid sense of curiosity piqued. "We used to share stories at night, my sisters and I, huddled beneath the blankets, long after the village went silent."

"You think me capable of such horrors?"

"I don't underestimate what your hands, or the other Elders, can do."

"I saw one once," Sorrell began, looking closely at Hyacinth to gauge her reaction. "A newly-skinned mask, fresh and steaming. It was carved perfectly, not an unnecessary tear in the flesh. Even I could admire its artistry, as blasphemous as it was."

"Whose face was it?" Hyacinth pressed. She found she was thankful it hadn't been Sorrell, that her husband had not slipped his blade beneath some sinner's skin and tore it away.

"Some girl whose name I never needed to learn. She was a heathen witch, unworthy of being known."

"And he took her face?"

Sorrell shrugged as if the awfulness could be so easily discarded. "And then we set the rest of her to flame. The mask, as perfect as it was, went to embers, too. Creating masks of heathen flesh is not something we condone, but it is not unheard of for an Elder to get carried away. Still. Such acts should not be tolerated."

"There is a line, then?" Hyacinth had always wondered what the limit of depravity was, what level of violence would be tolerated.

"It would seem so."

"You never answered my question." Hyacinth found her hand on her face, feeling the soft spoilt below her jaw. How easy would it be to peel her flesh back? To thread it with ribbon and peer out behind the empty holes where her eyes once lay? "What did you do, husband, for the blame to fall upon you?"

"Elder Lachlan found the letter and scared the others off. Then he gave me a choice, ever benevolent. Carry his sins and leave with you, or he would have Aviana hanged as a whore."

"You loved her."

"You sound disgusted."

"I think I may be."

"For falling in love or carrying the sins of another?"

He was still too close to her, all strange softness and quiet confessions. "Both, perhaps."

"This changes nothing between us."

Hyacinth knew that and understood it well. He would always be the man who stole her father from her, and she would always be his reminder of his sacrifice. Their sins, wickedness, and secrets were woven together, not in union but as chains, heavy and suffocating.

"Wouldn't it be easier if it did, dear husband mine?"

He gripped her hand, fingers tight around hers. Almost painful. The other, lingering at her cheek, drifted down to the pulse at her neck. Hyacinth tried to pull back, to sever the strange tension tightening between them. The sneer, ever-present on Sorrell's lip, fell, revealing a softness beneath.

If it was loneliness, curiosity, or a need for closeness, she did not know, would never know. But her lips parted all the same and met his. They came together in a clash of teeth and tongue, hungry and devouring as though they could be little else. They knew nothing else.

She bit into his lip, tasting blood, swallowing down the cry she wrenched out of him. His hair tangled, knotted around her fingers, and she dug in to force him nearer, to keep him still. Sorrell's hands raked through the knots of her own hair, his breaths panting, lips on hers, down her neck, slipping to the hollow of her throat.

And stopped.

They locked eyes, blood at their lips, hands entangled, hearts screaming. Hyacinth pulled away first, adjusting her skirts back down over her legs. She licked at her lip, dabbed it with a finger, and swallowed down the coppery tang that coated her tongue.

Sorrell pushed himself to his feet. "You kiss like a heathen."

"So do you." Hyacinth looked up at him, licking the blood from her teeth.

They stared at each other, chests still heaving, ragged breaths filling the void between them. Sorrell stepped closer, boots scraping her fingers. From where she lay, she could see his arousal through his trousers; it stoked her own, heating her.

"I imagine I fuck like one, too." Hyacinth leaned back, hand slipping beneath her skirts. Sorrell let out a choked sound, almost as though he were in pain. She half hoped he was.

His knees thudded to the floor, one hand grasping hers, wrenching them back behind her head. Hyacinth arched up, meeting his body as he fought to release his clothing. They met with a shared cry, bared teeth, and wide eyes. Sorrell's fingers dragged through the tangles of her hair, his mouth at her ear, teeth scraping her skin. Hyacinth clawed back, nails digging into his flesh, pulling him closer. She swallowed his moans, choking on her own.

Hyacinth twisted, forcing Sorrell beneath her. His hands tore through her lacings, palming at her breasts, hungry and rough. She let him, her head tipped back, knees clamped at his hips. She could still taste his blood on her tongue, feel the sting where his fingers tore through her hair. Blood and pain and pleasure all mingling into something almost sacred...or blasphemous, she cared little which.

A scream bubbled up from her throat, and it echoed, flooding the room and slipping beyond. Something else screamed back, beyond the woods, a song she had nearly forgotten. Hyacinth tore her pleasure from her husband, crying out with him. He shuddered beneath her, going limp and useless, her own waves of pleasure stretching far beyond his.

"We have a sacrifice to ready for," she said, removing herself from him coldly as if nothing had transpired between them. She leaned back on her hands, legs outstretched. "It would be a shame for us to be late."

Sorrell scrambled to his feet, smoothing out the wrinkles in his clothing. He left her on the floor as he walked away.

"You fuck like a heathen."

She looked up at him, licking the blood from her teeth. "So do you."

The scent of blood filled Hyacinth's senses, its warmth sticking to her skin and trailing down her cheeks like tears. Her mask was newly skinned, still soft, the ribbon piercing the hide silken and unfrayed. It filled her nose with the scent of death and new decay, trickling over her lips so she could taste it. No respite was offered from the stench of the mask, its closeness darkening the corners of her vision. Her breath quickened, and warmth slid down the back of her throat as she struggled to swallow.

She stood beside Mistress Yarrow, surrounded by the other Elder wives, all masked and silent. They were each bundled in cloaks lined with hare fur, as white as the snow that would soon come. A few of the Elders also wore the hides of foxes, heads lolling down over their shoulders like scarves. Their teeth glinted, yellow and sharp, their dead eyes wide.

In the quiet darkness, she felt fingers slip around hers and hold them tight. It had been Mistress Yarrow who tightened the ties of her mask, ensuring it sat right, so Hyacinth could see from the eye slits. Blood still coated her fingers, damp against her own.

"We must keep the village safe," Mistress Yarrow whispered. "This is the only way we know how."

"I know the sacrifice rites," Hyacinth answered, looking toward the circle of masked men and the torches they held. "I know how to feed the Teeth."

"But have you seen it?"

She thought of her father, the walk to the sinner's fence, the sight of yellowing bone protruding from the earth. She recalled the snap his neck made, the creak of the branches above.

"I have seen enough."

Mistress Yarrow said nothing but kept hold of Hyacinth's hand.

Mr. Douglas was led into silence, to bowed heads and dribbling blood. Hyacinth's heart beat so fiercely in her chest she feared everyone would hear the echo of it. A circle of bones lay ready for him, the picked carcasses of seven hares stretched out over the soil, bone to bone. Without a word, Mr. Douglas took his place in the center, sitting to rest his back against the oak in the circle center.

He was tied with plaited rope, strips of colorful ribbon sewn through, a piece of cloth from each household. Woven by the wives of the Woodsmen and the Boatmen.

"Are you a willing servant, Sir?" Elder Yarrow stepped forward.

"Aye."

There was a pause, a murmur before Elder Yarrow repeated, "Are you a willing servant, Sir?"

Mr. Douglas sighed, shifting his legs to stretch out in front of him. "By my flesh and bone, I am willing." He rolled his eyes. "Satisfied, you pompous twit?"

Elder Yarrow turned away, ignoring the old man tied to the oak as though he were lesser. Morgan's father was offering up himself in lieu of his son, as Hyacinth's father had done for her. The grounds were soaked in generations of blood, souls scrambling over themselves to give up their bodies for those they loved... The ground was so saturated in butchery, it was a wonder the Teeth were so famished.

"May the Oaks bear witness today," Elder Yarrow called out, his voice filled with a strange, almost giddy sense of glee. "The offering of flesh and bone, given freely this night by one of our own, by a son of the woods, of the Deep, of us."

"He is us," Hyacinth chorused, her eyes meeting those of Mr. Douglas.

He gave her a small nod. She looked away.

"Feast now and know we have repented. Take the bones and the soul, and swallow the sins we have committed. Let us be anew."

"Feast well." The words tasted sour, her sins lingering on her tongue.

They all wore them, were weighed down with them, but for all their falseness, the sacrifices did seem to appease the Teeth.

It was Elder Lichen who checked the ropes binding Mr. Douglas to ensure they held tight. He did so in silence, feet stepping over the steaming hares with a sense of care. His hand went to the old man's shoulder, giving it a quick squeeze before he backed away.

The wives walked away first, heads down, followed by the masked Elders with their torches in hand, leaving no light behind for Mr. Douglas.

"An awful business," Mistress Yarrow whispered to Hyacinth. "Say you will come back to my home for a drink to settle your nerves."

"My nerves are fine."

"Then to soothe mine, please."

It did not occur to Hyacinth that such a woman as Mistress Yarrow could feel the loneliness she did, the feeling of not quite belonging, as though all else were tethered down and the bindings knotted were frayed, broken, weak. She was always surrounded by the other wives or by the women of the village, hardly alone for a moment. She was so unlike Abelia, and Hyacinth feared there was little room in her heart for another, especially one who dared not speak her name.

"I will come if you raise a glass for Mr. Douglas," she said, slipping her mask up over her hair, streaking her hairline with blood.

"I will, Mistress Reed. I will."

Several Elders and wives walked back to the Yarrows' cottage, spilling through their doorway as though returning from a simple stroll. Masks were hung, cloaks strewn over chairs. Glasses were fetched from the cabinet, and before the first drink had been poured, laughter echoed around the damp space. It was a jarring sound, one that needled at Hyacinth. How any good humor or mirth could be had under such circumstances, she couldn't imagine. How could they recoil at the laughter of the wildlings, the heathens lost to the trees, their cackles high and free, but let such sounds fall from their own lips still covered in the damp sacrifice of an innocent old man? She knew the answer—those who made the rules surrounded her. Their laughter was sanctioned, holy, unquestionable. Because they said it was.

Elder Yarrow sat before the fire, his feet up and glass raised. He opened his mouth to undoubtedly boom over everyone else, but his wife cut in, her voice thin. There was a quiver to her words, though she held her chin high as she raised her own glass. "To the bravery of Mr. Douglas, we give thanks—"

"What on earth has come over you?" Elder Yarrow said, standing up so he towered over his wife. "Be quiet at once."

"I feel a toast to a dear neighbor is not out of line," Sorrell said, stepping up close to Hyacinth, his shoulder brushing against Mistress Yarrow. "The gentleness of a woman's tongue can be a balm against nights like these. Say that I am wrong."

He glanced at Hyacinth, the familiar curl of his lip lifting the edge of his mouth. She kept her gentle tongue firmly behind her teeth.

"Hear, hear," Elder Roan shouted, tapping his glass against the table. "Let us hear your prayers, Mistress Yarrow."

With her hands knotting in front of her, Mistress Yarrow continued her toast, her voice quiet but sure. She caught her husband's stare and kept it. "We give thanks to Mr. Douglas, a dear neighbor, friend, and father. We thank him for the gift of sanctuary, for the coming nights when we can lay down our children's heads and know we remain safe. Let us pray for his soul and that when no earthly body remains, his true essence lives on in neverending peace. May the Oaks bless him."

"May the Oaks bless him," they echoed. The words faded into silence, hanging over them, doing little to dispel the horror weighing against Hyacinth. The Teeth would pick him clean, swallow down his soul until there was nothing left to pass on.

The fireplace crackled, flames licking hungrily at the wood. Warmth filled the small space, almost stifling. Sweat gathered at Hyacinth's back, trickling down her spine. She moved closer to the window, staring out as if she could see Mr. Douglas from the cottage. There would be nothing warming his bones that night, nothing of comfort or softness save for the bloodied shirt upon his back.

Dim candlelight flickered in the corners of the cottage, settling into the cracks in the wood, over the embroidered linen on the table, the lace at the windows. Drinks were passed freely: dark port in small glasses and the last of the summer ale in silver tankards. Hyacinth sipped at her blackberry wine. It was sticky on her lips and not strong enough to dull the restlessness threatening her. Apple cake sat on plates decorated with clusters of purple aster, dark berries glistening on top, honey drooling from the centers. It was all too sickly, thick with a decedent sweetness, filling the air until Hyacinth thought she would vomit.

"I need to take some air," Hyacinth said, catching the swaying arm of her husband. She had watched him pour drink after drink down his throat with the rest of the Elders. Whether it was to keep up with his peers or to drown out the imagery of Mr. Douglas, she had no way of knowing. Mistress Yarrow stood in the far corner of the cottage, surrounded by the other wives. She did not look up to see Hyacinth take her leave. "I'll see you back home."

His hand caught her sleeve, lips wet at her ear. "Don't be seen going to that man's house in the dark."

"I am not so foolish."

"Keep the blasted dog with you."

She poked him, and he swayed. "Careful now, husband. You make it seem you are concerned for my welfare."

"Imagine that."

Hyacinth snuck out of the cottage and its strange mix of aloofness, laughter, and intoxication. She did not wander toward Morgan Carroway's home, not to check on him, nor to fetch her dog. Instead, she followed the dark and winding pathway back into the woods to the shadows and the Teeth and the silent, waiting form of Mr. Douglas.

She said nothing as she settled among the ancient oaks, the wet moss soaking through her skirts. She was unsure whether he saw her coming to wait with him if he knew she had come and that he was not alone.

Darkness hung over the trees like a blanket, snuffing out the stars. Hyacinth pulled on her mask, the blood long dried, now cool on her face. She had no circle of bones, but she sat still all the same. Still and silent. The old familiar chill dread did not come to her.

Hyacinth's heart beat a steady thumping in her chest, and her breaths remained even. There was a calmness where once her fear had settled, but though she strained her ears for any sign of the wildlings' song, the air around her remained quiet. It was silence, a bated breath, and nothing more.

Then They came through the shadows, slicing Their way through the darkness. The earth rumbled, cracked, shook. The hanging bones rattled. Mr. Douglas looked up, his eyes stretched so wide, it was a wonder they remained in his skull. Talons cleaved the soil, and the low guttural cries rebounded off the trees, the awful sound scratching at her ears.

Hyacinth watched, frozen, as the Teeth took pieces of Morgan's father. A taste, slow and lingering. One finger and a scream, another and another. They bent over his body, snapping bone, savoring the middle as though They had all the time in the world. His screams quietened, slipping into whimpers, into tears. They feasted on the sins, and They gorged themselves.

And she watched.

CHAPTER NINETEEN

Hyacinth slipped back through the darkness, away from the splintered remains of Mr. Douglas. Bones lay against the mighty oak, wet and scratched, their marrow leaking across the damp soil. They would be collected by the Woodsmen, cleaned and consecrated, carved and hung to keep away the Teeth. To remind those what the Teeth could do, how They feasted so deliciously on the sinful.

The chill bit into her, curling fog caressing her skin. It tangled in her hair, tendrils almost like fingers, calling her back. She should have gone back to her cottage to curl up and warm herself by the fire with the cushions that smelled like her. She wondered if Sorrell knew she was missing, that she hadn't gone back, or if he was too drunk to notice her absence. She doubted he would be concerned for her welfare. Most likely, he worried more about what scandal she would bring upon him by wandering around in the dark alone.

Although her cottage called to her, home was a place nestled so deep in her chest that she had to fight to recall it. It was not the fog-soaked place around her, the damp wood, and the sound of the waves. It was her childhood home. This place was not hers, and it left her feeling untethered, a transient soul with no place to truly call home.

Lost to her thoughts, she hadn't realized she was trailing along the path that wound to Morgan's cottage. He was far from home, but she knew she could share quiet grief with him, both knowing the appetites of the woods with sharp clarity. She arrived at his door but did not knock.

"Take off your fucking mask."

She opened the door to see Morgan in an armchair, the darkness solid around him. No flames warmed the hearth, no candles were lit to hold back the shadows. Faolan lay at his feet, his head on his knees, his dark eyes shifting to the doorway. A quick thump of his tail let her know he was glad to see her.

"If you're coming in, leave that thing at the door."

She yanked it from her face, feeling the bindings tear. She scrubbed a hand over her face in an attempt to remove the blood. From the look on Morgan's face, she knew it was still there, dried and ruddy over her cheeks.

"I came by to say I stayed with him through the end." Hyacinth stepped further into the dark, moving to stand beside his chair. "He wasn't alone."

"You should not have done that."

"No one saw."

"You are so certain?" His voice was flat, eyes red. "They already whisper about you, Hyacinth."

"And do you? Do you whisper about me?" She settled herself on a stool, fingers running through the coarse fur of her dog.

"No one would listen."

There were tear tracks on his face, deep shadows beneath his eyes. A tankard of ale sat next to him on the small table. He looked smaller, hunched over, fingers curled into fists in his lap.

"And if they did?" she asked softly, needing his answer. To know that there was someone...anyone who saw her.

"You are a wicked thing," he said, not looking up.

Hyacinth rose, swallowing down the spark of pain in her gut.

Morgan's hand shot out, fingers gripping hold of her arm. "But I think you have to be, for yourself, so no one can tell how scared you truly are."

"What have I to be afraid of?"

He laughed then, a quick burst of sound. "You do not fear the gallows."

She pulled her arm away. "You are drunk."

"Aye." Morgan reached for his drink, emptying its contents down his throat. "So tell me, Mistress Reed. Was my father granted a swift death?"

"Morgan..."

"Or was he pulled apart slowly? Flesh ripping, innards steaming while he screamed?"

"We exist in darkness," she whispered, unable to find the right thing to say to bring comfort. There were no such words but how she longed for their taste. "Would you like to keep Faolan?"

"He is yours. I would not take him from you, Hyacinth."

"It's because he is a massive brute, isn't it?" she said playfully, hoping to pull him away from his bleak thoughts, if only for a moment. "You would inflict a beast such as he on me, knowing he takes up half the room and eats enough for a small family. Generous indeed, Mr. Carroway."

He laughed, a quick spark of humor erasing the harsh lines on his face. Then he crumpled, a sob following the echo of his laughter, breaking past his lips with a gasp. He fell forward, face in his hands, folding in on himself as though to hide it all from Hyacinth.

She never did well with such displays of emotion. Briony was prone to them and would often be comforted by Celandine while Hyacinth looked on in uncomfortable silence. But she placed a hand on Morgan's shoulder, pulling him close like she had seen her sister do many times before. It seemed enough. He buried his face against Hyacinth's shoulder, his tears quieting.

"Do not stain my dress with your crying, Morgan Carroway," she said softly, smoothing the hair from his face. "This is my finest one."

He pulled back with a soft smile, running his palm over his eyes and cheeks. "You give shit hugs, Hyacinth." He took a slow breath and held it, calming himself.

She remained close, almost touching, though not quite. They breathed the same air, the darkness and the dampness of the room folding over them both. She was unsure who moved first, if they both fell, without thought or reasoning into the other. A gravitational pull. His kiss was soft and slow, tasting of tears and liquor. She drank it down, pulling him closer, her teeth at his lip. With one hand, Hyacinth tugged up her skirts, the other fumbling for the buttons on Morgan's trousers. He groaned into her mouth, fingers slipping against her hip.

"You are married," he breathed, words tasting of sin and shadow.

"You don't say."

"They'll string us both up for the crows."

"You're shit at sweet-talking women, Morgan Carroway." She kissed him again, her hands sliding lower and lower until he was nearly boneless beneath her. His mouth slipped to her neck, tongue at her throat, at her ear.

They startled at the knocking, the dull sound echoing across the room with a damning thud. Hyacinth settled her skirts a moment before the door swung open.

"There you are!" Mistress Yarrow said, stepping into the dimly lighted cottage. "My dear, I have been fretting."

"I..." Hyacinth fought to compose herself, glad for the low light so Mistress Yarrow couldn't see the disarray she was in. "I was just..."

"Oh, I can see!" Her boots clicked against the floorboards as she walked forward, steps quick and stern. She gripped Hyacinth's hand, holding it tight. "How thoughtful of you to look into Mr. Carroway on your way home and to bring him more broth." She nodded to the stove, where the thickened cold remains of Mrs. Mormor's soup still sat. "Heat it up," she hissed.

Hyacinth yanked her arm away, moving in silence to heat the

soup. Mistress Yarrow came up behind her, taking the spoon from the pot to splash it over Hyacinth's good dress.

"Why did you do that?"

"No one will believe you cooked without making a mess of yourself, dear."

With the soup beginning to bubble, Mistress Yarrow pulled Hyacinth from the cottage like a wayward child. She stopped once to address Morgan. "Don't leave that to burn the house down, and for the love of the blessed Oaks pull your trousers up!" She took a breath, sucking it between her teeth. "I am sorry for the loss of your father, Mr. Carroway."

Hyacinth tripped over her feet as she was dragged by Mistress Yarrow, one hand still gripping hard around her fingers, the other draped across her shoulder, pulling her close like they were embracing.

"This is twice now that I have needed to cover for you. Do not allow there to be a third." The words were hushed, only for her. "I am your friend, Mistress Reed. Believe that if you don't believe anything else, but I will not take a noose for you."

Hyacinth flinched, forcing herself away from the smell of smoke and herbs on her breath and clothes. "I never asked you for it— your help or your friendship."

"But you have it anyway!" Mistress Yarrow allowed her hands to drop. "Because you sorely need it."

"Was I missed?"

An almost smug smile flitted across Mistress Yarrow's mouth, though her eyes remained hard. "As fortune would have it, you were not. The others joined my husband in depleting our liquor stocks. It was quite the sight. I escorted Sorrell home but could not get him up the stairs, so he's on the sofa."

"That is twice now you have called my husband by his name,

Mistress Yarrow," Hyacinth said, watching her smile vanish. "And yet you refuse to use mine."

"Forgive me... I partook in a few glasses myself..."

"Indeed." Hyacinth untangled herself from the woman's shadow, from her lowered gaze and too-bright eyes. "Goodnight, Mistress Yarrow. And thank you again for your discretion."

Hyacinth walked the rest of the way home alone, taking a moment to stop and stare into the woods. She thought if she stared hard enough, she would see them; if she just strained harder to hear, their song would find her. Silence was her company. Even the wind had stilled.

She stared and stared into the darkness, and nothing stared back.

Her cottage was dark, the fire reduced to embers. Snores rumbled from her sofa, the body beneath her blankets still and slumbering. Hyacinth peeked at him, shoving him without care onto his side. He drooled over her favorite cushion, embroidered by Celandine for her wedding day. Hyacinth snatched it from his head and stormed upstairs.

She missed the companionship of her dog, the presence of another soul under her roof that cared for her. That minded not the wickedness in her heart nor the heathen thoughts dancing on her tongue. She had yet to hear him howl to the trees, and a small part of her wished he would so she could see who, what answered. If the echo would draw her in again, an outstretched hand of bone, or if it would solidify her fear, causing her to turn her back on the woods completely. But she would not begrudge Morgan the comfort Faolan gave him, hoping that perhaps the hound would bring him solace.

The scent of her husband lingered on his blankets, on the pillows, all dried herbs, and woodsmoke. Hyacinth stretched out a hand across the mattress, feeling set adrift. It was comfortable, soft, and cocooning. She would not be giving it back.

"We sleep side by side, never touching, or you sleep outside, my dear!" she called down, voice echoing. She doubted he heard her in his drunken slumber, yet she felt better for voicing it. Claiming it.

The hours passed, but sleep did not find her. Her skin pricked with heat, almost fever-hot. She could feel the echoes of Morgan's lips on her neck, feel the bruises of his kiss, the gentle exploration of his eager fingers. It stirred her heathen heart, the wickedness inside, leaving her restless and wanting. She closed her eyes, hands trailing the path he had traced, following the curves of her body just as slowly, with the same reverence. It was a different sort of worship, a slow blessing, a caress of her fingers and her mind. Her heart beat a hymn, singing a crescendo wholly unfamiliar to her. She arched, a gasp falling from her lips, body twisting in the sheets. A different warmth flooded through her, one of calm and contentment, of relief. She settled back against the pillows, and sleep found her, cradled her, and left her dreamless.

The waves crashed against the rocks, soaking Hyacinth's boots as she slipped her knife through the fresh fish and tossed its bones to the side for carving. She stood with the other women, their hands busy, wild hair caught by the wind. Mistress Roan sat near her feet, one hand slicing through the fish in her lap with skilled hands, the other around Mistress Vanora, who sat quite still, her gaze unmoving from the distant shadows of the trees.

Hyacinth did not know the woman well. They had only exchanged a few pleasantries when working down by the water, but her smile had been kind enough. She had a laugh that swept over you, gentle and warm. There was no trace of it now, and any softness on her face had bled out, leaving it hollow. Hyacinth had not witnessed the wrapped bundle of Melantha's remains handed to her mother, but she had stood at the hole in the ground and watched her be lowered in. It took three wives to keep Mistress Vanora standing, from throwing herself into the cleaved earth to join her daughter's bones. Her husband had stood still, unmoving, silent. The prayers chanted by the others went unrepeated, as though he had lost faith in them.

"We haven't enough," Mistress Yarrow whispered, the words drowned by the relentless waters. "There are gaping holes in the nets... There aren't enough fish."

"I wove them tight—"

"I know." Mistress Yarrow reached for Hyacinth's hand, her fingers wet with brine. "I know you did. But the Deep is angry."

"Will there be a storm?" Mrs. Merla asked, her bright eyes turned to the waters, knife clutched tight. "So soon after the Teeth?"

"The waters are rough; that is all, a warning, nothing more." Mistress Yarrow looked to the other women, voice rising. "We take the flesh, we carve the bones, we feed the Deep."

"We feed the Deep," came the echo.

Clouds rolled in over the waters, turning them an inky blue. They swelled with rain, bringing in distant rolls of thunder. The water grew restless, waves inching higher, tearing close to the rocks where Hyacinth sat. She shifted her skirt, her shoes already wet, and fixed her stare on Mistress Yarrow.

"Looks like a storm to me."

"I have seen worse," Mistress Yarrow answered, though her voice shook. Hyacinth could hear the lie, felt it unsettle the others. Comforting words were of little use. "Get as many fish in the baskets as you can."

Rain began to fall, a fine mist that clung to Hyacinth's skin and clothes before seeping through to her skin. She half-wished it would just pour and be done with it. Her knife slipped, the blade sloughing through the flesh of her finger. She saw the blood before the pain hit.

"Oh goodness!" Mistress Yarrow caught her wrist, stemming the flood of red with her skirt. "You must take care, Mistress Reed."

Hyacinth stiffened at the tone, not liking being scolded like a wayward child. "You said to hurry."

"Without taking your hand off, dear." Blood seeped through the cloth, dripping onto the damp stones at their feet. "Does anyone have a clean rag—thank you, Mrs. Fern."

The older woman handed over a white piece of thick linen, sliced neatly from her own apron. She took Hyacinth's hand from Mistress Yarrow, and began to wind the clean strip tightly around her finger.

"Get that cleaned as soon as you can," Mrs. Fern said gently, squeezing Hyacinth's fingers. "Else they'll be eyeing up your finger bones."

"That's enough of that." Mistress Yarrow wiped at the blood on her skirts, frowning when it didn't budge. "Are you feeling faint, my dear?"

"I've not swooned once in my life, and I shalln't be starting now."

Her palm ached, a dull throb that wound its way up her arm and to her shoulder. With a grimace, she flexed her fingers, feeling the torn skin pull beneath the bandage. Tears pricked her eyes, but she quickly blinked them away before Mistress Yarrow could see them. She didn't want the pity.

"The boats!"

A cry rumbled down over them, nearly stolen away by the growing waves.

"We are sending out the boats!" Sorrell clambered down the sodden steps, his mask in hand. "Ready the oars."

"You cannot be serious!" Hyacinth stood, hands and clothes bloodied. "The waves will tear the boats down, forget what else may hunger for their souls."

"We send the boats, or the famished waters will rake through this village and take its fill!" He pushed past her, snatching up a crate of skinned fish and hauling it to one of the boats. The

Boatmen joined him, racing down the steps without a care, their feet solid and sure.

"What are you doing?" Mistress Yarrow rose beside Hyacinth. They both watched as Sorrell sat himself in one of the boats. "You are no Boatman. Get out at once."

"Elder Yarrow wishes for one of us to go out, to keep the sacred words close, to say our prayers directly to the Deep."

Hyacinth looked between her husband and Mistress Yarrow. "Why you? You are new to the village. You have never been on a boat."

"Perhaps it is a test," he answered, taking in her bloodied state, her wild hair, and clothing ragged by the wind and waves. What he saw in her then, she did not know, but it looked as though it frightened him.

"You are a fool if you go," she hissed.

"And a coward if I stay." He grabbed for the oars. "They will not burn you as a witch but hang you for being a coward's wife."

"Better the noose than the flame."

"Dead is still dead, my dear."

"Stop this quarreling!" Mistress Yarrow forced herself between the boat and Hyacinth, hands outstretched. "Have some grace, the both of you."

"You think he should go then?" Hyacinth asked, still bristling.

"It matters not what I think..."

"That says enough."

"I should have wed the other sister," Sorrell hissed, words low enough for only Hyacinth to hear.

"Celandine or Briony?" The names of her sisters caught between her teeth, slipping past like spittle. "Neither would have brought you happiness, I assure you."

"I cannot imagine a worse fate than you, dear wife..."

"I can hear your blasted bickering from the west path!" A voice echoed past them, and they turned as one. "You'll have the tongues wagging again."

Morgan took deep strides over the rocks, his boots crunching over the smaller pebbles. He folded his arms, eyes narrowed.

"What business do you have here, Mr. Carroway?" Mistress Yarrow asked, hands scrunching the folds of her apron.

"My own, Mistress," he answered, stepping over to the boat. The wind snatched at the red stands of his hair, his face beneath unshaven. "Move over then, Elder Reed. Let us feed the Deep."

"Have you both lost your fucking minds?" Hyacinth sputtered.

"Who bid you to go, Mr. Carroway?" Mistress Yarrow said, ignoring the foulness of Hyacinth's tongue. "You have the marks of a coward if you beg my pardon, but you are tainted, Sir."

"A fine way to honor your father," Hyacinth began. "To give yourself to the Deep."

"I know these waters, Hyacinth," Morgan snapped back. "Shown to me as a boy. Your husband does not."

"Then you are both fools."

She turned on her heel, blood still trickling down her arm, and walked away. Not once did she look back, not to the scrape of wood over stone, not at the crash of waves or the call of the Boatmen. She walked and walked and walked until she felt the tug of her sleeve.

"Mistress Reed..."

She whirled. "I beg of you, leave me alone!"

Mistress Yarrow flinched but did not back away. "I thought we could wait together and whisper our prayers to those who might listen."

"Perhaps it is a shame that I was wedded to Sorrell and not Briony," Hyacinth said. "I feel she would have been suited to your friendship. She would have bored him; there is no doubt about that. Though I do not think that would have mattered really, do you?"

"I do not know what you mean..."

Hyacinth nodded, glancing toward the waves. "Go swallow your sins, Mistress Yarrow. Leave me to choke on my own."

CHAPTER TWENTY

D ark clouds bled out over the skies, blotting out the weak sunlight, tempting the shadows deeper into the village. The winds blew in hard, whipping the hair from Hyacinth's face and snatching the edges of her cloak. It battered at her windows, shaking the glass until she was sure it would shatter. She had to force the cottage door closed, leaning heavily against it as the wind howled behind her. She bolted it, standing in the center of the room, breathing tight. The wood creaked, the bones above clicking and spinning, the threads binding them becoming knotted.

She would not think of the Deep, of the huge monstrous waves, of the hunger that lingered beneath. Not think of her husband, of Morgan, of the Boatmen sent out on those devouring waves. Would they come back at all? Or would they be consumed, taken, kept, like the Woodsman? Drowned and knotted with weed, barnacles on their skin, throats filled with silent screams and sand?

With shaking hands, Hyacinth lit the lanterns, fixing them firmly to the hooks so they didn't tumble, and set the house alight. Her finger ached, the bandage sodden and dirty. She rummaged through her scant supplies, working in the wavering candlelight to find fresh gauze and a tin of ointment. She would be damned if anyone would take her fingers while she still drew breath.

Her hand cleaned and bound, Hyacinth felt in her pockets for the familiar smoothness of her father's finger bone, checking it was still there, nestled close. She wondered if she should carve it, but she couldn't bring herself to press her knife against it, to scrape it, to etch it into something other than her father. She gave it a squeeze; knowing it was there would be enough.

She yearned for a good cup of tea, something warm and comforting for her hands to hold. But the wind followed her, slipping down the chimney, screeching and whirling, and sending up ashes. It doused the struggling lantern light, sending shadows up the walls. Hyacinth sat in darkness, pulling blankets around her, wondering if she would be swept up, house and all into the storm.

A harsh banging at her door forced her thoughts back, her nerves in tatters as the dog at her side began to bark. She shoved Foalan aside and threw open the door, nearly blinded by the lashing rain. It screamed on its hinges, bending, almost snapping free.

"Are you quite mad?"

Mistress Yarrow stood at the threshold, soaked and shivering, hands clasped to keep her cloak from flying away. She should have looked in a pitying state, standing on Hyacinth's doorstep with mud on her face and her golden hair in tangles. Yet she stood fierce, eyes hard, fingers clutching the door frame with grim determination. For a moment, she looked like a part of the storm, a wild thing, and Hyacinth wanted to tell her so, knowing well it would wound her.

"You must come to the Form. It is not safe here—the Deep will come."

"I am far enough from the water, I think."

"Please..."

"Go back before you are swept away," Hyacinth demanded, grabbing Faolan by the scuff to stop him from clambering for the doorway. "Leave me to withstand this storm in peace."

"I beg of you." Mistress Yarrow clutched the doorframe harder, planting her feet against the growing wind. "It will come for you here, please...please, Hyacinth, come."

The sound of her name should not have moved her in the way it did, settling in the small part of her that longed for friendship, to belong. She scowled back at the drenched woman, fingers tightening on the neck of Faolan. He growled, but she did not release him.

"Fine," she conceded. "If it will move you from my doorstep and save me the trouble of explaining how you stood here and drowned, then I will come."

"We must make haste!" Mistress Yarrow dragged Hyacinth from the cottage before she could say another word. Faolan stayed close by her legs, teeth nipping at her fingers as though to quicken her steps.

Above them, the sky loomed a heavy black, full of bloated clouds spilling torrents down upon the earth. They could no longer see the paths. Hyacinth could barely see Mistress Yarrow in front of her. The wind screamed, snatching at their voices. Hyacinth clutched her hand, fingers scratching. Mistress Yarrow's fingers scratched back as though, together, they could keep their feet on the ground.

Hyacinth tumbled, her feet catching something solid. Her knees bruised as she fell, but her cry was swallowed up, the bandage on her hand flying free. Grit and dirt pressed into her flesh, mingling with the fresh wound. Mistress Yarrow landed beside her, mud on her legs and in her hair. Her eyes widened, and without a word, she began to drag herself backward.

"What—" Hyacinth turned, eyes landing on the solid thing she had fallen over. A scream lodged in her throat, choking the air from her until she thought her lungs would burst. She could make no sound, could not move. Her bones lay tethered to the sodden earth, and she feared she would never rise.

The wooden post was nearly lost in the mud, like a sinking ship, the end rising as the ground slowly swallowed it. The remains of the unwed lay scattered, the ropes binding them knotted with seaweed, slick and blackened. They had been hauled from their resting places by the furious winds, taken far from the outskirts of the village to sprawl their desecration at the Elder's doors. Crows had not yet finished their feasting. The skull jutted from the wood, still with flesh, gray and stringy. Wet. The eyes were gone; they were always the first to go. Hyacinth could see the spine, a window of vacant skin. Hair spilled out in tangles, an awful rusted brown. There were traces of softness still lingering in the curls, fragments of ribbon.

"They were swept here by the storm," Hyacinth said, needing to speak before she did nothing but scream. "Look at the things we do!"

She stood, taking a moment to feel the bruises on her skin, the scratches, to feel the echo of horrors around her, around them. Some posts had splintered when they hit the earth, spilling bone and decaying skin. They fell in a circle, some upright, as though they had always been there, sightless eyes staring down, jaws loose. Others lay scattered, bones tumbling together until they were no longer one person, one body, but a mass of pieces.

"It is what we have always done..."

"Does that make it right?" Hyacinth screamed then, her words raw, aching. She breathed in the pain. "Mistress Yarrow?"

"We must get to shelter." Mistress Yarrow pushed herself to her feet, her face beneath the filth stark white. "Else the Deep will surely take our bones."

"It would be no less than we deserved," Hyacinth murmured, but the wind did not snatch those words from her. She saw the moment they landed on Mistress Yarrow's ears, saw the curl of her lip, the narrowing of her brow. How much, she wondered. How far could she push her before all threads of their friendship were severed?

Mistress Yarrow snatched Hyacinth's hand, her fingers rougher than before, her hold painful, hard enough to leave bruises. Hyacinth didn't pull away but dug her nails deeper into the woman's skin. Together, they continued to push through the storm, their skirts and boots soaked and heavy, the howls of the wind and the roar of the waves close behind them. So close. Too close.

Hyacinth reached the great oak door first and dragged the handle forward so they spilled into the Form, into their salvation, away from the Deep.

Voices filled the room, frightened and tense, bodies packed in tight. Candles wavered pitifully in the draft. Hyacinth was ushered in and met by the warm hands of the Elder wives, the wives of the Woodsmen, the Boatmen. Scalding hot tea was pressed into her hands, and a warm blanket draped over her shoulders.

"Where on Earth were you?"

"Blessed Oaks, girl, you're soaked to the skin!"

"You cannot wait out the Deep from your home, Mistress Reed."

The voices barreled into her, heavy with concern.

Then Elder Yarrow stepped forward, mask tied to his ruddy face. "I have every faith your husband will return."

"May the Deep spare him." Hyacinth shook off the chaos of well-wishers. "May the Deep spare them all."

"The Teeth have feasted on our sins, given to the Oaks by the body of Mr. Douglas—now the Deep is famished. It reaches out, seeks to feed on the sins we did not cleave."

"What sins remain here, then, Elder Yarrow?" Hyacinth asked, feeling warmth slip back into her hands from the mug of tea.

"I fear the greatest one of all, Mistress Reed." Elder Yarrow bent low, words brushing against Hyacinth's cheek. "I fear we have a witch amongst us."

She did not flinch. "How awful."

"Do you remember what we do to witches, Mistress Reed?"

"Aye." She met his gaze, eyes watering at the tang of liquor on his breath. "Burn their bodies and carve their charred bones. I paid attention to my sermons, Elder Yarrow."

"Are you a witch, Mistress Reed?"

Hyacinth waited for the echo of gasps to disperse; some

villagers stepped back, away from her. Others drew closer. The firm hand of Mistress Yarrow curled over her shoulder.

"Goodness, Elder Yarrow!" Hyacinth splayed a hand over her heart. "To utter such words to me, to cast such accusations at me when my own husband braves the Deep. We are all so very frightened—the storm comes, and it comes for us all. Do not let your fear tie lies upon your tongue."

"We are not yet certain a witch is to blame here." Elder Lichen stepped forward, forcing Elder Yarrow down onto a stool with a firm shove. "We pray for the safe return of your husband, Mistress Reed, and for all those out over the Deep."

Hyacinth smiled at the thin, spider-like man. He hovered over Elder Yarrow, ensuring he did not get back up and would remain quiet. There was a glint in his dark eyes of want and lust...though it was not directed at her. He whispered something to Elder Yarrow, whose ruddy cheeks went pale, the color leaching from his skin before her eyes.

CHAPTER TWENTY-ONE

T he storm screamed through the Form, rain lashing against the glass. The howl of the wind tore the thatch from the surrounding cottages, snatching the lanterns from their hooks. Flames scattered to the ground, quickly spluttering out over the soaked grass. It was a small mercy, one Hyacinth held close; they would not burn. She would not burn.

They cowered together beneath the solid roof of the Form hall. The Elders sat on their dais, overlooking them all, their masks down, faces hidden as though neither the Teeth nor the Deep wouldn't see the men beneath. Hyacinth sat on the cold floor with a young girl a little older than Elstren huddled in her lap. Her mother sat beside her, nursing a babe at her breast, keeping her other two children close by, their hands locked together.

"My dada," whimpered the girl, golden curls hiding her face. "My dada."

"My father was a Woodsman," Hyacinth said, holding the child closer, feeling her heartbeat flutter against her chest. "He kept the paths safe, carving and hanging the bones. He stayed out when night fell to ensure the trees remained rooted and that hunger did not slip out into the village. I would wait for him just as we wait now for your father."

"But it is so dark…"

"It was dark in the forest, too. Sometimes, the wind would come and steal away the candlelight, just like tonight. I would try to light the lantern, but dark it remained. My father always came home."

"You left him behind to come here?" Her little voice was muffled by Hyacinth's dress, her tears soaking through the fabric. It seemed a good place to cry.

"Aye, just as you will one day."

As they all did, tied to someone not of their choosing, sent out into the dark, through the hungry Teeth, to a place unknown to them. Share the stories, keep the faith, bring the bones, carve the bones.

There was nothing beyond that.

Water seeped beneath the doors, bringing with it weeds and grit. It rippled over the wood and pooled at their feet, ice cold and black. On the wind, against the lashing of rain and the branches against the glass, they could hear the screams of the Deep. A hollow sort of noise that echoed out over the village and shook the hall.

They huddled closer, heads low, voices whispering prayers over and over as though they would be heard over the din of the abyss. A few eyes turned to her, hardened by Elder Yarrow's accusations. She wondered how many it would take to drag her from the hall, to toss her to the waves, the Teeth, the Deep, to see if she sated them at all.

Hyacinth's bones ached, her feet wet from the relentless sea. They were all sodden, the waters lapping at the edges of the benches they stood upon. The raised wooden dais remained dry, which would no doubt be considered a blessing in the eyes of the Elders, rather than it being an extra few feet from the waterlogged floor.

But the storm had quieted. Drawing back from the village with a howling scream, it left nothing but black water and fear behind, taking nothing else.

"I will head down to await the Boatman," Hyacinth called out, holding up her damp skirts as she jumped down from her bench. "If the Elders permit it?"

"We will also go," Mistress Yarrow said, hopping down beside Hyacinth. "The Elder Wives and the wives of the Boatmen, to see them safely home."

"May the Deep have been merciful," Elder Lichen said, leaning down with steepled fingers. "May it be only a gnashing of teeth, a warning to keep our sins checked, and a reminder that we are here only by the grace of those far larger than ourselves."

Hyacinth caught Elder Yarrow's eye, and he scowled down at her from behind his mask. He had no words for her, no accusations. Nor did he have any for his wife.

"If those remaining behind would see fit that there is tea and something hot to fill the stomachs of our brave men, it would be met with much gratitude." Mistress Yarrow looked out over the villagers, ensuring her voice was heard. When there came no dissent, she took hold of Hyacinth's hand and walked from the hall.

"You are hurting my hand," Hyacinth hissed, forcing her fingers from Mistress Yarrow's. "I am walking right beside you. There is no need to grapple at me!"

They passed the circle of unwed, the posts still swaying in the breeze, splinters of wood and bone scattered over the ground. Hyacinth could not help but stare, to wonder if the taste of timbre would have scratched her tongue had she denied Sorrell. Would her mother have tried another boy, someone kinder, someone she could grow to like who might like her in return? Hyacinth would never know the answer; her mother had gone weeping to her husband's death and not uttered a word to stop it. She wanted to know, to ask her, to carry a mother's love close enough to her heart that there was no doubt.

"Do you think they are safe?" Mistress Yarrow asked, looking forward, eyes fixed on the path ahead and not the pieces of flesh and bones on the posts.

"It matters not what I think, does it?" Hyacinth replied, beginning her descent to the shore with care. Though the rain had stopped and the clouds had dissipated, the wind was still fierce. It whipped at her hair, at the scarf holding Mistress Roan's ebony curls, and at the woolen hat atop Mrs. Merla's head. It snatched at them all, desperate to take even the smallest pieces of them. "They are either coming home, or they belong to the Deep; hoping and wishing will not change that."

"You are surrounded by Gods; will you not pray to them? For the safe return of your husband, your...friend, the other men out there? Do you fear they do not listen?"

"Oh, I know they listen. That is why I do not pray."

The sea was a calm mirror, soft and sparkling with the early sunrise. There was a beauty to it, which made it all the worse. "They eat our prayers as they eat our sins," Hyacinth continued. "They eat our flesh when they please and only pretend to follow the rules—"

"Stop it."

"Do I frighten you, Mistress Yarrow?"

There were tears in the other woman's eyes, slipping down her cheeks. "Yes."

"I am not sorry for that."

"Do you like being alone, Mistress Reed? Do you think if you close yourself off, make yourself unlikeable, untouchable, you won't feel pain?"

"I am doing quite well—"

"But I see you," Mistress Yarrow pressed, her gaze fixed on the calm horizon. "Who did you lose? Who did the Teeth take from you?"

Hyacinth's lips formed around the name, but she swallowed the sound of it. Guilt, hot and heavy, pressed against her, calcifying around her heart so she felt leaden. She was sure that if she flung herself into the Deep with the sins she carried, she would plunge straight to the bottom.

"The boats are coming back," she said, pointing to the dark shadows far out over the sea. "The men are coming home."

The women hurried to the shoreline and waded to their knees in the frigid waters. Their skirts floated around them as they reached for the knotted ropes of the boats to haul them back to shore. Quiet descended upon them as the faces of the men came into view. They were silent, wide-eyed, and pale. The only sounds to be heard were those of the lapping waters and the panting breaths of the women hauling the boats in. One boat was missing.

Hyacinth pushed through them to the small vessel holding her husband and Morgan, Mistress Yarrow closely behind. They aided the men onto the stones and led them up the steep, slippery steps back to the village. Hyacinth held tight to Sorrell's arm, his blue and frozen fingers gripping her skin. His clothes were ripped and torn, blood running in rivulets over his arms, scratches crisscrossing over his skin.

"What happened?" Hyacinth held Sorrell fast, keeping him upright when his knees began to buckle. "Where is the other boat?"

She turned to Morgan, who was blue-lipped and pale. There was blood on his hands, but she could see no wounds.

"Gone, Mistress," another Boatman murmured behind them, his arms tight around that of his wife. "Swallowed down."

"Just the one?"

"Aye, the others remained untouched."

They led Sorrell and Morgan to Hyacinth's cottage, watching as the other Boatman slid away to their own homes. They had seen horrors before, from the Teeth, from the Deep, from the Elders themselves with their hangings and burnings and sin feeding. They had often returned to shore quiet, saddened, tired. But she had not seen such frozen terror before; there was a new sort of hopelessness to it.

Her cottage was full of seawater, glass from shattered windows floating on top. It trickled down the stairs while weeds and mud sluiced up the walls. It was as though the Deep had consumed it and spat it back out.

"What a mercy it is that you left with me, Mistress Reed." Mistress Yarrow pushed past her, lifting a few chairs from the floor. She set them right in the puddles of brackish waters and forced Morgan and Sorrell down on them. "I dare say you would have been whisked away."

Morgan looked up sharply, a strange noise bubbling from his throat.

"Do you tire of gazing down at us from your high horse, Mistress Yarrow?" Hyacinth asked.

"Not in the slightest," came the reply. "The candles are all soaked through, and it will be impossible to light a fire here for days, maybe weeks if the weather is unkind. Do you have any whiskey?"

"If there is any left, it will be in the top cupboard."

With Mistress Yarrow rummaging through her wet cupboards, Hyacinth crouched down beside Sorrell, pushing up the tattered remains of his sleeves. His skin was raw, covered with vivid lines that bled freely. Where the skin had been torn, it was also bruised. She held her hand over the gouge marks, her fingertips nearly fitting the wounds.

"The Deep did not make these." Hyacinth plucked the bottle of whiskey from Mistress Yarrow, splashing it liberally over Sorrell's arm. He did not flinch.

"He would not let go..." Sorrell said, his voice trembling with his body. Everything about him shook. There was no bite to his words, no familiar cutting remark, no sneer. He gripped hold of Hyacinth's hand as though he were drowning, and only she could pull him free.

"The waves took the boat—took the fish and the bones— dragged it all down. It spat them out—it spat them out, Hyacinth! The bones and the Boatmen! They were covered in weed and scale, eyes white, mouths gaping wider than a man's jaw should ever be.

They cracked, jawbones hanging from flesh that looked like it had seen weeks of the Deep, not mere minutes... They grabbed our boat, their keening cries screeching across the storm..." He trailed off, voice giving out.

Mistress Yarrow thrust a mug of whisky into his hands, tipping it up towards his lips.

Morgan held his own, fingers clamped around the edges, his hands shaking enough to spill the amber liquid onto his lap.

"I dragged him away." Morgan took a sip, choking as it trembled down his throat. "But the Boatman would not let go. He was something deranged—possessed, grappling for saltless skin. I had to snap his fingers, and he still fought to bring your husband down with him."

A silence fell over the damp darkness, silent echoes of horror drifting like smoke around the room. It clung to them, chilling their bones.

"By the blessed Oaks, you made it back," Mistress Yarrow said into the quiet, her voice soft.

"There is no blessing." Sorrell looked up, having drained the last of his drink. "Those two men were taken by the Deep, screaming into the storm with their jaws hanging loose, weed around their necks like nooses. And then it calmed. Like smoothing wrinkles from a scrap of cloth as though nothing had happened—"

"It laughed at us." Morgan lifted his mug for more, and Mistress Yarrow refilled it without saying a word.

"When the waves had gone quiet, and the sun burned again above us, it laughed."

"What did it sound like?" Hyacinth leaned forward to comfort or to hear better; she did not quite know.

"Like it could swallow worlds."

CHAPTER TWENTY-TWO

T he cold seeped into Hyacinth's cottage, cutting and unforgiving. Though the water receded, everything was left damp, and without the promise of a summer's sun to dry it out, they would all remain cold. The storm had reached upstairs, soaking through the bedding, the pillows, and the chest of Hyacinth's belongings. Everything lay ruined, and it was little consolation to find that Sorrell's things were ruined, too.

"One night in this bed," she hissed, tearing the saturated quilts from the frame. "One fucking night! Look, it's already growing mold."

Mistress Yarrow looked on, her hands clapped together. If she wondered why Hyacinth did not share a bed with her husband, she held it in. "We will make you new ones, my dear. I have yet to see my own cottage to see if it withstood the storm. If it has, if the Oaks saw to bless us, we will find space for you beneath its roof."

"You still think yourself blessed?"

"The men came home..."

"Who were your prayers for, Mistress Yarrow?"

"For all the souls who took to the Deep."

Hyacinth added her good dress to the pile of sopping clothing and bedding before reaching out for her wedding dress. Brackish water had stained like veins across the silk, the delicate lace frayed, the ribbons torn. She held it for a moment, remembering her mother's hands as she gently pinned the hem, ensuring the dress fell perfectly at her feet. It had been the only time she had seen her mother look at her with any softness, with a hope that Hyacinth would be good.

"What are you doing?" Mistress Yarrow grasped for the bundle of muddied fabric and tossed it into another growing pile. "This may yet be saved. We can trim the silk and make a lovely nameday dress for your daughter—"

"I want it burned with the other things."

"My dear," Mistress Yarrow began. Her words were cut off by the look Hyacinth threw at her.

She cleared her throat. "As you wish. If the men downstairs are well enough to be left, I think it is our duty to check to see if any cottages were swept to sea. I dare say Mr. Carroway's—"

"Faolan!"

The cry rebounded about the cottage, startling Mistress Yarrow and alarming Sorrell enough that his mug slipped from his hands. It landed on the soft, wet floor with a thud.

"I left him sleeping on the bed..." Morgan said, standing quickly as Hyacinth made to run from the room. "Wait!"

"You left my dog!"

"You forgot about him!"

"My dear," Mistress Yarrow said, scooping up the mug to place it back in Sorrell's hands. "Let me come with you to look. There may be hope yet."

Hyacinth looked to the woman, then to the wide-eyed stare of her husband. He still trembled, his breathing hitching, catching as though his lungs could not quite let in enough air. There was no love in her heart for Sorrell, not even loathing, but she pitied him, and his suffering did not comfort her the way it should have.

"No. You stay with him before he keels over."

Then she pointed a finger toward Morgan, who scowled back at her. "My dog better be okay, Mr. Carroway."

She did not wait for him to answer, hearing his footsteps follow behind her as she rushed out the door. The village was as soaked as her cottage, pieces of it lying like driftwood on the sodden paths. Window frames lay caved in, shards of glass buried beneath the receding waters glinted in the scarce light. Above, the skies were still thick and heavy, allowing only a little sunlight to bleed through. No houses had escaped the fury, most bent inwards, all exposed beams and torn roofs, half devoured and drowned. Hyacinth's boots slipped in the thick mud covering the pathways, heels crunching the fragments of glass, the pieces of bone ripped free from their hangings.

She spotted Morgan's cottage ahead, teetering at the cliff's edge, and hurried toward it.

It looked as though the Deep had risen and plucked the cottage from its foundation. It hung, swaying gently at the edge, its thatch covered with debris and blackened by water. It clung to the beams, all sodden straw and tangling weed, flapping over the great holes in the roof like sliced skin over a wound.

"Faolan!" Hyacinth called his name, straining in the still air for any sound within the crooked mess of beams and rotten thatch. The bones hanging from the shattered porch clicked together, hanging on by the barest of threads. She watched as they clicked and clacked before the rope that bound them finally snapped, and they plunged over the cliff.

"It is going to fall any moment!" Morgan grabbed her arm, hauling her back. She fell against his chest, feeling the solid thump of his heart beneath her own. "If you go in there, you will fall with it."

"Then I had better be quick."

"Hyacinth, it is not safe!"

Anger swamped her tongue, so thick she could taste it. "Nor was rushing out into the Deep!"

"I went to ensure your husband did not drown, that he came home."

She glared at him, all the things she wanted to say locked behind her tongue. He looked at her as though he knew the sound of her silent words. If he judged her for them, she could not quite tell.

Hyacinth pulled away, saying nothing. She ran to the yawning door, its hinges rusted thick, clinging to the frame by cobwebbed pieces of red metal. The wood beneath her feet was slick with seaweed, bowing with the weight of the water, inches deep and murky black.

"Faolan!" she called again, straining to hear anything beyond the groaning of wood as it clung to the edge of the cliff. And there, in the dark, she heard it. A whine, faint and pained, coming from above her.

She ran to the stairs, which sunk the moment her feet stepped on them. The wood had rotted through, but they held. She did not give a thought to if they would hold her and her dog when she came back down. Up she went, her feet slipping, hands gripping the sodden banister. Everything tilted and shifted under her. She paused, holding her breath, teeth at her lip, heart in her throat. She heard the whine again, the soft, low keening of something pained. Hyacinth moved faster, feet slipping over the slime, to Morgan's bedroom.

The bed lay in ruins, its wood snapped, the headboard plastered to the wall by a web of green. The window frame hung loose, shards of glass glinting across the floor like pieces of sand. She saw the matted gray of a leg, then the larger body of her dog. Caged within the remains of the bedframe, the wet straw of the torn mattress cradled him so it looked like a nest. The bedposts bowed over, near joining in the middle.

He watched her with eyes big and black, not moving as she crept closer until her hand landed on the scruff of his neck.

"Good boy," Hyacinth whispered, pushing against the wooden posts. They bent and snapped with ease, allowing her to pull Faolan free. She held him close, and he let her, his head pressing into the crook of her neck, his nose cold and wet against her skin. She cradled him, breathing in the scent of damp and saltwater, of firewood and grass. He smelled like home, and it made her cling to him tighter.

"Make your way slowly back to me."

Morgan's voice came up behind her, and she turned her head, barely moving. The floor beneath her creaked and moaned.

"Now, Hyacinth."

"Take the dog." She nudged Faolan toward him, watching the floorboards begin to split beneath his massive paws. "I'll follow."

Morgan gritted his teeth, his body rigid and eyes dark and angry, but he crawled forward all the same, his large hand coming around to catch the scruff of Faolan's neck. He dragged the dog away, ignoring the whines and yelps he made. Faolan's teeth snapped close to Morgan's fingers, and he all but pushed him down the stairs.

"Now give me your damned hand, you mad woman!"

She remained still for a breath, listening to the howling of Faolan below her. She could feel the splitting cracks, the water-logged floorboards giving way beneath her. Hyacinth reached out, her fingers brushing against Morgan's hands. She felt the calluses of his palms, the coldness of his touch, the desperate reach of them.

But she fell all the same.

She was in the woods, soil beneath her feet, seawater in her hair. Abelia stood over her, her neck crooked, bone pressing through her skin. Moss grew over the wound, up over her throat to her cheek. She smiled, her lips stretching wide, tendrils of vine spreading from her mouth to the black of her eyes.

"Take my hand."

The words rasped over her split lips, showing the yellow of her teeth.

"Come with me, Hyacinth."

"Where?"

Hyacinth was cold, a strange sort of cold that made her bones heavy. "Where do I go?"

A hand stroked over her face, the skin brittle and damp. "Home. Come home, Hyacinth."

"But it is so far away."

Abelia's bones clicked as she settled beside Hyacinth, her skin stretching like old cheesecloth. She leaned closer, her breath of moss and rot brushing against Hyacinth's cheek. "It is right here. It has always been right here."

Her mouth closed over Hyacinth's, her lips cold, tasting of blood and dirt. Hyacinth swallowed the earthen musk, allowing it to take root within her.

"Come home..."

"Come back to us," another voice said over her, sounding close. It drowned out the sound of Abelia, warming the chill of her touch. "That's it. Open your eyes, dear."

Hyacinth blinked against the candlelight. She lay in bed, one that was not her own, covered in blankets pulled high. On a stool to her right sat Mistress Yarrow. She heard footsteps fade into the distance and the sound of voices wafting up from below.

"You gave us quite the scare," Mistress Yarrow said, dabbing Hyacinth's forehead with a damp cloth. "All for that monstrous beast."

"Morgan?" The name fell from her mouth, cracked and raw.

"The dog, dear."

"Is he..."

"Both are well." Mistress Yarrow kept her voice low. "You were dragged from that house half dead. By the mercy of the Oaks, you were not crushed."

"I fell."

"Through the bloody floor and then nearly off the cliff." The woman pursed her lips, looking vexed at the curse that slipped so quickly from her mouth. "If Mr. Carroway had not been there, I dare say your body would have been claimed by the Deep. He brought you here covered in blood—both of you covered—screaming with that damned hound braying at his heels. I thought Hell itself had come to scourge us all clean."

"Imagine that." Hyacinth shuffled so she sat up against the soft pillows. Her body ached. "Where am I?"

"In my home, dear."

Hyacinth followed Mistress Yarrow's gaze, taking in the sloped ceiling, the simple bed, and the woven rug. "A room meant for our children, though alas, we have yet to be blessed."

Hyacinth caught the tone, the sharp edge to her words. "This world is not built for children," she said softly, thinking back to the child whimpering on her lap during the storm.

"Perhaps not."

Mistress Yarrow stood, smoothing out the folds of her skirts. They were wrinkled deeply as though she had sat beside Hyacinth's bed for a long while.

"I'll fetch you some tea," she said, tucking the blankets around Hyacinth. "And tell the others you are awake."

"Has he asked after me?"

"He does not wish to see you dead, Mistress Reed."

It did not answer her question. She wondered if Sorrell was one of the voices she heard from downstairs and if he waited to see if she would wake.

Tea was brought to her, yellow and bitter, alongside a steaming bowl of something gray and lumpy. Hyacinth took the cup, sipping gratefully, the warm liquid soothing her sore throat. She pushed the bowl of soup aside, not having the stomach for it.

"Mrs. Mormor's fish broth will see you right." Mistress Yarrow lifted a spoonful to Hyacinth's lips. "It tastes better than it looks, I promise you."

Hyacinth licked the spoon with caution, unable to trust the other woman not to shove it in her mouth. It was thick and salty but not terrible.

"I want to go home." She ate another few bites to show her health had returned. "I think I am okay to go home."

Mistress Yarrow pressed a hand to Hyacinth's shoulder, guiding her head back to the pillows. "Your cottage is in ruins, my dear. You need to stay here, where I can look after you."

A warmth spread over Hyacinth, making the tips of her fingers tingle. The weight of the blankets grew heavier, the softness of the pillow behind her head pulling her down into a velvet darkness. "I want to go home..." she slurred, her words thick and useless. Her eyes closed against her will, the cool dampness of a cloth pressed against her forehead.

"Hush now, my dear. Let me take care of you."

CHAPTER TWENTY-THREE

T ime passed in a strange blur of dreams and half wakefulness. At times, Hyacinth swore she felt the press of Abelia's ruined fingers over hers, smelled the warm rot, the sharpness of forest pine and soil. But it was the solid form of Mistress Yarrow she would wake to, damp cloth in hand, bitter tea close by.

"I pray you forgive me," the whispered words drifted over her, as insubstantial as smoke. "That the Oaks will forgive me. Let the Teeth not taste my sins, Hyacinth. I beg you."

Hyacinth blinked away the gumminess from her eyes. She was unable to lift her head up, but she turned to Mistress Yarrow. "Why?"

"I will keep you safe. Let me keep you safe."

"From who?" The words fell as soft as cobwebs, drifting away before she could finish them. A part of her knew who, but that piece of her was too far away.

"Hush." Mistress Yarrow pressed a hand to Hyacinth's lips, head snapping around to the doorway. "Close your eyes."

"Has she woken?" A deep voice filled the small space. Hyacinth could feel the woman beside her shrink away. "Has the witch risen at last?"

"She sleeps still, husband," came the reply, the words trembling. "But she is a witch by rumor only, not because you declared it to be so."

"I am not the only Elder who believes she is something wicked. The Teeth and the Deep are famished, unsated since she arrived."

"Are there souls upon your council who think otherwise?" Mistress Yarrow asked, her fingers finding Hyacinth's and squeezing gently. "Are the Elders decided? Will they take her bones? Hook her for the Deep or string her up for the Teeth?"

There was silence for a moment, and the darkness threatened to pull Hyacinth down, away. She fought to remain in the gentleness, a pillow at her head, warm blankets over her legs. She missed such comforts, missed the sure hand of another woman, soft like her sisters.

"We cannot count the vote of her husband; he would hang right beside her."

"And yet you do count it," Mistress Yarrow said, her voice growing steadier. "It still bears weight, even though he would never testify against his wife. As an Elder, his voice is still law."

"You think you know all..."

"I listen." The chair legs scratched against the floor as Mistress Yarrow stood. "Now, who else?"

"Elder Lichen." The name was spat like a foul taste.

"That surprises me."

"It should not. It is to sow discord, nothing more."

"You wonder why the world is so very hungry for us. It is for the heavy sins we carry, for the rot here."

"Hold your tongue, wife, before I have it removed."

There was the sound of footsteps and a hand at Hyacinth's chin, fingers harsh. "You spend too much time with this heathen creature. I will not have my name sullied because you are weak of mind."

THE BONE DRENCHED WOODS

"I do my wifely duties, do I not?" There was a sharpness to her voice Hyacinth had not heard before. It suited her.

"I care for the sick and needful. Even the sinners. It is to show that I am merciful and unafraid so that they may look at you and see you are not afraid."

"There is one duty you have failed me in." The hand at Hyacinth's face dropped; she could still sense him above her, the smell of liquor warming the air. She held her breath until her lungs burned. "My name is to be remembered here, my legacy sent out through the Teeth, over the paths. I will not be forgotten."

"The Oaks may bless us yet," Though hushed, Mistress Yarrow's words did not falter. "Have faith in me, as I have faith in you, in the prayers we speak, of the goodness we keep within our hearts."

"My faith has been tested of late." The heavy footsteps of Elder Yarrow moved away, nearing the doorway. "It is no easy task, wife. To feed the Teeth and the Deep, to keep them both sated, to keep the sins that flow over these thatched roofs, these sinful creatures. I remain a devout man. Do I not deserve my just rewards?"

"It is not for me to say what you may or may not deserve."

"No, it is not."

The floorboards creaked with his retreating footsteps, the sound slipping down the stairs and away. Breath shuddered through her lips; her cheek was still warm from Elder Yarrow's angry hands. She forced her eyes open.

"Do you pray to the Oaks, Mistress Yarrow?" Hyacinth murmured. "To bear that awful man a child?"

Mistress Yarrow reached for the teapot steeping nearby, pouring the bitter liquid into a cup before pressing it to Hyacinth's lips. "Aye, every night, every waking morn."

She kept the cup to her mouth, pressing firmly so the warm tea spilled down Hyacinth's chin. "And the Oaks have blessed me. I am blessed. Now drink your tea, dear."

Brutal hands dragged Hyacinth from her bed, snatching her from a slumber so deep she wondered how she had awoken at all. Her hip struck the floor, her nightdress bunching around her legs. She stared up, blinking through her wavering vision. Elder Yarrow stood above her, a foul grin slashed across his face. Elder Lichen stood at his side, silent and pale. Hyacinth couldn't read him; he looked neither pleased nor alarmed. She turned, searching in the low light for her husband, but Sorrell was not there.

"We shall find out tonight where your bones will lie, Mistress Reed," Elder Yarrow rasped, crouching low, his wet lips casting spittle at her ear.

Despite the bruises forming on her hip and her knees, Hyacinth met his stare, refusing to blink, to look away. "For which crime have you decided?"

"Oh, we will find one that suits you."

Hyacinth was not permitted to dress, and she shivered as she was led down the stairs on weak legs and forced out into the frigid night.

Only the Elders gathered, masked and waiting. It reminded Hyacinth of her father's hanging, how there was no trial, no mercy. The chill soaked through the thin layers of her nightgown, slipping into the bones beneath. Hyacinth bit her lip to stop it from trembling, tasting blood.

"The hunger has stirred since your arrival here, Mistress Yarrow," Elder Roan began, the scales on his mask catching the moonlight. "No one can doubt that. Are you a witch?"

"I am not, Elder Sir." Her voice faltered, fear weighing her words down, so they fell clumsily from her bloodied mouth. She hated how they could see her tremble, hear her tremble.

"Your husband has also testified that you are no witch. His words matter, Mistress Yarrow."

"Do mine?"

"Not enough." Elder Roan took her hand, almost gently, and led her onto the wooden platform. "You know that, Mistress Reed."

Hyacinth couldn't run, not with her useless legs and swimming mind. Even if she could, would they simply shoot her down like Emory Merrow? She was suddenly a child again, watching in horror as the woman ran for her daughter.

"A hanging then?"

She searched the small group for Sorrell but could not find him. She was thankful he would not see her swing; she could not bear if his smugness was the last thing she saw.

"There is an *otherness* to you, Mistress Reed, one that does not fit in here. It sings to the Teeth, to those who hunger for us, if you mean so or not. What are we to do with you?"

Hyacinth would not beg them, would not get to her knees on the hard earth and scrape for her life. She said nothing and waited.

"A hanging and a stripping of bone," Elder Yarrow murmured to Elder Lichen, nodding his head so his jowls trembled. He was as keen to see her sway as her husband was. Beside him, Elder Lichen stood silent and still, his too-bright eyes fixed on Hyacinth. "Perhaps," he said, lips staining into a thin smile. "I would like to hear what Mistress Yarrow has to say."

They turned as one, fish masks shining, the smell of oily rot heavy on the breeze. Mistress Yarrow stepped forward from the shadows, her cloak pulled tight, her hair whipping wildly around her wind-chilled face.

"You would hear my voice," she said, stepping closer, "but you would not hear hers?"

Elder Yarrow blustered, face a livid red.

Elder Roan placed a hand on his shoulder, forcing him back. "Speak quickly," he demanded, casting a wary eye to Elder Lichen.

"Allow me to bear witness to Mistress Reed's character, to the good I know she carries. If I am proven wrong, take my bones as well."

"The Teeth are close," Elder Lichen said, gesturing to the trees. "They have been promised sustenance this night."

"Then take something from her, but let her keep her life."

A finger, they decided.

Hyacinth stood on the hanging platform, the noose swaying so close she could almost feel the roughness of the rope. The Elders, in their grim masks, huddled together, deciding which piece of her they would take. It was quick, too quick.

Before she could cry out, they grabbed her.

Elder Yarrow took her wrist and sliced deep, the bone beneath crunching under the blade. Tendons sprang, and her veins dangled as blood, red as fury, rushed down her arm.

She watched, breath sticking, heart pulsing with the flow of blood. Three fingers were hacked away, falling to the wet earth with barely a sound. Her heartbeat roared in her ears, the cold dark becoming too bright...too loud. Hyacinth felt herself fall, felt the noose she had narrowly escaped rub against her arm.

And then, there was nothing.

Hyacinth woke to wavering candlelight, a glow that didn't quite reach the corners of the room. She peered into the shadows, outstretching her hand to the rolling dark. She could hear the footsteps, the shuffle of bare feet, of bone on wood.

"Abelia?"

The name croaked, a scratch against her throat. Hyacinth slipped from the bed, sinking to her knees as the room spun. Her stomach turned, and she let a dribble of bile spill from her lips. "Are you here?"

She crawled in the dark, knees bruising as she pulled herself toward the window. The frigid air settled over her flushed skin like a balm. She needed the light from the window like a gasp of air, a final heartbeat, needed to drag back the heavy curtain to bring moonlight so she could see. She needed to see Abelia, see if she had come for her at last.

The curtain fell back easily, and moonlight trickled in, banishing the shadows. Nothing lingered in her room. Grief and guilt knotted her heartstrings. She wanted to curl inward, the ache in her chest sharp. It was a different kind of alone, something other.

Then she heard it.

Heard it again.

Bone over earth—not wood, not the floorboards, but well-trod earth. Gripping the windowsill with her good hand, she heaved herself up, arm shaking, sweat pooling down her skin, over her spine. Her other hand was in ruins, bound tight, bloodied wrappings leaking.

They came in slowly, together, the four of them. Their boots were gone, for they had been lost to the waves, the sound of their steps unnatural, shaking the earth. Four Boatmen, with flayed skin and sodden bone, followed the winding pathways, leaving a trail of water and seaweed in their wake. From their open mouths came a song. It was so unlike the call of the wildlings, the women in the woods, that Hyacinth had once so readily run toward. It was a keening cry, a rasping sound that had Hyacinth cowering behind the glass. It was fear and drowning, a cold promise. There they stood, strings of netting peeling with their skin, fish scales glittering in the moonlight, blood and brine gleaming on their remains.

She did not make a sound—could not make a sound—as they called forth their wives, their sons and daughters, from their sleeping beds. Cries joined the awful song, neighbors shouting from behind closed windows. No one stepped over their thresholds. Hyacinth stood at hers, gripping the sill, her breath fogging the glass as she watched and did nothing.

Their families walked forward willingly; Hyacinth could see that. Eyes open, arms outstretched, unflinching when the slick, flesh-striped arms embraced them. And they were led away, back to the cliff, into the darkness, the rasping song dying out. Hyacinth didn't move, didn't dare open her window, yet she heard them fall. For a moment, the waves quietened, allowing the screams to carry back to the village. Small screams, quick and then lost, like falling pebbles.

The fevered sweat cooled on Hyacinth's skin, and she shivered, her fingernails leaving scratches on the windowsill. She stared, listening to the roar of hungry water of the fathomless Deep. Lights flickered from the neighboring porches as everyone waited and watched, silent. No one moved.

"My dear."

The door creaked behind her, and she jolted, world spinning. "You should not yet be up."

"Did...did you see?" Hyacinth took a step toward Mistress Yarrow. "The Boatmen..."

"Yes."

She fought not to faint. She was not some swooning maiden, but she was fevered from her mutilation, and it was a weakness she was loath to share. But down she went, knees cracking the floor. Her head fell upon softness, the scent of honey and lavender filling her senses. It smelled like her mother, her sisters, of home.

Was she home?

Darkness drifted over her, a blanket of warm nothingness, and she stopped fighting.

CHAPTER TWENTY-FOUR

H yacinth listened to Mistress Yarrow's slow breathing. Bitter tea clung to her lips. She wasn't sure how much time had passed nor how much longer she would be kept in bed. She felt the lack of dignity like a scrape to a wound, being cleaned and dressed as though she were a doll.

Her ears pricked at the sound of footsteps, turning to watch the silhouette slip across the wall. She opened her mouth to speak, but her tongue lay too thick and useless in her mouth.

"Hyacinth?" The sound of her name brought the sharpness of tears to her eyes. "Can you move at all?"

Morgan stood over her, resting one hand on her shoulder and the other at her cheek, turning her head to face him.

She tried to shake her head, noise bubbling from her lips in a pale mimicry of words.

"I came to see you over and over, but they would not let me in," he said, fingers tracing the curve of her jaw. "I pleaded to Mistress Yarrow—begged her, you will delight to hear—for a warm place to lay my head. My cottage, as you know, slipped into the Deep." He spoke slowly, paying little heed to the slumbering woman beside them.

Mistress Yarrow slept on, her mouth open and snoring.

"Your friend is very clever. No one else suspected she was keeping you asleep here." He held her gently, with a strange reverence. "But I watched her steep your tea. I made sure to brew a large kettle full of her 'special herbs' for her and the others. They won't wake for a while."

"What...?"

Morgan caught the look on her face, the flash of fear that she was too tired to hide.

"I'm getting you out of here, Hyacinth," he said gently. "I cannot sit back and watch you wither away in this bed, no matter the intentions of your host."

"Where..."

"To your cottage. It is still damp and awful, but you can't stay here." He brushed the hair from her eyes, his touch lingering. "You will need to try and walk. It needs to look as though you stumbled home. Can you do that?"

She forced her head to nod, feeling her neck creak with the effort.

Morgan heaved her from the bed, his arms tight around her body as she fought to bring life back into her limbs. Her feet scraped along the floor, and her head hung loosely from her neck. She was a marionette, strings pulled tight with no say where she was led.

A dull ache pulsed up her hand around the absence of her fingers, but it was not the bright, slicing pain she had felt before. Hyacinth twitched the remains of her hand, feeling the ache tighten beneath the clean bindings. The rips in her flesh were healing.

"How..." the single word grated at her throat, the sound little more than a rasp. "...long?"

"A month, maybe a little more than that," Morgan replied, pulling her close for a moment, his lips at her hair. "I tried to get to you."

And she believed him.

"Down the stairs," Morgan said, telling her where to place her feet. He kept talking, not allowing silence to hang over them for long. "Be careful. Can you manage the handrail?"

Hyacinth had enough strength in her neck to look at him, hoping he could read the annoyance in her eyes, see the curl of her lip.

He looked back with a crooked smile. "I can only guess at the quips blessing your tongue, Hyacinth." He tightened his hold on her, taking most of her weight as she ambled down the stairs. "Silence does not suit you."

They managed to stumble from the cottage out into the frosty night. Clouds formed where her breath panted out. The village was quiet, its shadows still and watching. Although it had long passed, broken beams and shattered glass still lay across the paths, glittering among the frozen grass like snow. The storm had laid waste to the village, leaving it in ruins. The posts had been taken away, the bones tied to them removed, the brittle pieces of the bodies taken elsewhere. If they were tossed to the Deep or strung for the Teeth, Hyacinth did not know. She did not ask. Pieces of dried seaweed still clung to the path. It had dried in the sunlight, curling inward, blackened and reeking.

The Drove, from what Hyacinth could see, stood near untouched, its great oak doors still standing, windows whole, the bones hanging above white and clean.

"Maybe it is truly a sacred space," Morgan said, feet crunching over the lingering sharp fragments of the houses pulled beneath.

"No." Hyacinth swallowed, forcing the words past her lips. "What use is it to drown us all?"

Morgan stood for a moment, his eyes on the Drove and his arm tight around Hyacinth's middle. She caught her breath, stretching her back, her arms, her legs—all her bones until they clicked. She could finally feel her body, its weight, even if she could not yet quite control it. Her tongue loosened, and she unclenched her jaw.

"Do you think they will come again?"

"If they do, the Deep or the Teeth, I fear there will be no saving you, Hyacinth."

"I did not do this."

"I know." He brought his head towards hers. "There is something rotten within this village, and they can sense it."

"The rot that wears masks and speaks such lovely, sacred words?"

Morgan sucked in a breath. "I can almost taste the blasphemy on your tongue."

Hyacinth shifted closer, her mouth brushing his, teeth against his lip. "And what does it taste like?"

He kissed her slowly, tasting her, his hands drifting up her back to her hair, tangling it in his fingers. "Like the trees," he breathed the words, and she swallowed them down. "Like a wildling."

"Like a witch?"

He pulled away, eyes bright, his hands still knotted in her hair as though he was loath to be parted from her. "Like you would eat this world if given the chance."

The smell of damp and wood rot filled the cottage, and the fireplace was dark and empty. Wind whistled through the glassless windows, but the shards had been swept away. Someone had at least attempted to tidy up the ruins of Hyacinth's cottage. Before leaving, Morgan lit the few candles that escaped the worst of the storm, and though he tried to light the fire, there was no dry wood. He had found her one almost dry blanket, and she settled on the damp sofa with Faolan by her side. The dog bore no real injury save for a swollen paw and a cut to his muzzle; it had scarred over, reminding her of the time passed by.

She slumbered, half listening to the heavy breaths of her dog, listening out for the sound of the door opening. She wondered if she would be dragged back to Mistress Yarrow's spare room, declared unfit to care for herself, or dragged to the pyre instead.

Hyacinth opened her eyes to the sound of footsteps, her body numb from the damp and cold rather than from the bitter tea forced upon her. Sorrell stood in the doorway, boots creaking over the slowly rotting floor. Hyacinth sat up, one hand resting on Faolan's neck.

"Do you not feel foolish," Sorrell said, placing the lantern in his hand down on the table. "For risking your life for that beast?"

"Not in the slightest." Hyacinth swung her legs around so she sat facing him. The damp blanket slipped from her lap and pooled on the floor. "It feels right to risk all to save something so free of sin. We would feel the lack of it if I let him fall."

"You speak of yourself?"

She shrugged. "I am just as burdened with my share as you."

"They will not set you to the flame," Sorrell said, stepping into the scant light the lantern offered. "You have me to thank for that."

"Only because they would use you as kindling right beside me."

"I know that man helped you here tonight." Sorrell folded his arms, leaning against the wall as if he cared little. The tightness of his stance, the tension of his jaw, the coldness of his eyes told Hyacinth otherwise. "You are not to see him again. There will be no more talk, no more whispers of how my wife has caught the eye of another. Do you hear me?"

She smiled. "But then will talk not turn to you, dear husband? Of your wandering eye and roaming hands."

"I have not the faintest idea what you are talking about."

"Oh please, hypocrisy ill suits you, as does playing the fool." She stood, her legs chilled from the dampness of the sofa. "What would Elder Yarrow think to know you have been rutting his wife in the darkness, in the shadows?"

"You dare..."

"Oh, I dare." She closed the gap between them, words hot. She could taste their fury, lingering fear, and desperation. "You seek to threaten me, to force me to obey your word and be meek and good, and yet you forget that I know your secrets, your heart, your sins. I will not go down quietly, Sorrell. You will gain no honor in my death."

"And what of Alona?"

A soft laugh fell from Hyacinth's lips. "You say her name with such reverence. Mine never sounded so from your mouth."

"Would you risk her life? Her soul? To reap your retribution on me?"

"You cannot lay all the blame on me," she hissed, her anger a steady thing. "I am not a vessel to which you can stuff full of your sins and remain innocent. Any retribution you face will be of your own doing, that I promise you. If it wounds those dear to you, know you dealt the blow. Your hands are stained red."

He moved quickly, one hand at her throat, the other pressing the tip of a blade close to her ribs. Faolan lunged, his yelp tearing through the darkness as the flat of Sorrell's boot came forcefully onto his side.

"I will have your silence, or I will have your life, Hyacinth," he hissed, face too close. "I have let you live..."

"Let me?" She shifted, scraping the knife against her skin. "I can feel your hand shaking, husband mine. What are you afraid of?"

"I do not fear you."

"The Teeth, then?" Hyacinth felt her throat bruise. "The Deep, as well. You heard it, the laughter, that insatiable appetite for misery. The endlessness of it all. Do you hear the singing? Hear it from the dark, the shadows, the Oaks? I can hear them singing, Sorrell."

The knife drew back, clattering to the wooden floor. "Witch."

"How could I be anything else?" She moved her misshapen hand upward, folding it over the one latched to her skin. "I was never given room to become anything but."

"I won't let them burn you—I'll not go to the flame, you hateful thing!" His teeth were close to her mouth, spittle at her cheek. "Grant me your silence, or I'll smother it from you."

"What is to stop you?" She did not flinch, did not try to loose the hand at her throat. "If not tonight, why would you not snuff out my life while I slept, toss me down the stairs? Carry me to the Deep and throw me out?"

"My word."

"Oh, aye?" The words stuck in her throat, rasping past her teeth. "Blessed am I for the small mercies of men."

His fingers squeezed, eyes flint sharp, lips drawn back. With one hand, he pressed, nails digging in, pinching her skin. Her breath caught and failed. Hyacinth lunged forward, her teeth snapping fiercely. She took his cheek, all soft skin, and tore it back.

And he howled, a piercing shriek that she gasped down like she gasped air. She spat at his feet, a globule of red along with a small, tender strip of flesh.

"Heathen whore..."

His words bubbled, mouth gaping. Hyacinth pulled back her hand, leaving behind her father's finger bone in her husband's neck. She watched him a moment, watched the disbelief and fear slip over his face. Then she wrenched the bone free, and a spray of blood followed, warm and sticky. Her grip slipped, hand fumbling with the lack of fingers, but still, she brought her hand down, again and again, into his soft flesh, her scream joining his, fury and agony blending into a sweet cacophony.

Hyacinth knelt on the floor, careful not to soil her dress on the blood soaking across the wood. Her corset was soaked, dripping scarlet, but her skirts were clean. How proud her mother would be.

She wanted him to see, to know that it was no accident, not sudden rage. His eyes, those lovely eyes, met hers, drifting down to her hands. She traced his cheek with the fingerbone gently without breaking the skin. And with a sigh and a small smile, she bent forward and kissed his brow, words ghosting over her bruised throat.

"For my father, you worthless fuck. May the Oaks bless you."

CHAPTER TWENTY-FIVE

H yacinth sat on the damp floor of her cottage and watched the life dribble from her husband. Faolan sat close, the gray hair on his paws soaking up the red. He whined, low and quiet, chest rumbling. It was the only sound in the house, save the long rasping gasps of Sorrell. They silenced after a while, and the dog grew silent, too.

Hitching her skirts up, Hyacinth took her husband under the arms and began the slow, awkward shuffle of dragging him from the cottage. Her hand throbbed with new pain, the bindings soaked with Sorrell's blood. The dog followed, tail low, eyes shining in the moonlight. She was glad of the company, of the knowing look he shared with her.

Into the woods she went, silent and strong, head held high. Hyacinth's fingers grew numb in the bitter cold, but her heart lay lighter in her chest. The shadows swallowed her up as the bones tied to the trees clacked above. The paths were overgrown, almost gone, devoured once again by the Teeth with no one left to clear them. She wondered how long it would take for the Teeth to nibble at the edges of the village, to choke it down, until there was nothing left at all.

With care, she propped Sorrell against one of the twisted oaks, fastening his mask over his face. There would be no circle of bones for him, no words of protection. She folded his fingers over one of her good knives, though she hated to lose it, but it all needed to look convincing if she was to keep her neck intact. With it, she folded a note, the paper taken from his desk, his penmanship copied.

And she left him. Left him to slowly rot, become mulch for the famished roots, or be consumed by those with hungry mouths. It mattered little to her. He was gone.

They came for her in the morning, granting her the kindness of a knock on the door rather than forcing it from the hinges. She had scrubbed the floor and tossed her muddied skirts into the fire, so any proof of her misgivings burned and not her. She washed the blood from her hair and dressed in a clean nightgown while Foalan watched on. If he judged her or approved of what she did, she could not quite tell. She removed the filthy bandage and tossed that, too, into the flames. New flesh shone in the vacant space where her fingers once were, the edges jagged and red but clean. She imagined her bones had been stripped and carved, and she wondered whose home they dangled in.

In the end, all the blood and filth washed away. It was so very easy to wash away.

"It is early, Elder Lachlan. Elder Roan," she said, opening the door after the third knock. "What brings you to my door at this hour?"

Elder Roan shifted, hands fiddling with the knot of bones on his belt. "We need you to come with us, Mistress."

"There has been a rather awful incident concerning your husband." Elder Lachlan held out the note. Blood had made it brittle, the edges tearing.

The slow stab of fear was real enough, and Hyacinth's heart quickened, making her still and silent. If they saw it as guilt or sorrow, only time would tell. Tears were of no use to her. Even if she could conjure them up, they would look out of place on her cheeks.

Hyacinth was given time to change into something decent. Though a part of her wished they allowed her to stand in the Drove in her nightgown if only to see the scandalized faces of the Elders. She was escorted silently from her cottage, her footsteps crunching on the frost-stiffened grass. Dawn barely lit the far edges of the village. A cloud of mist hung heavy and cold around her ankles like ghostly hands reaching out. Inside the Drove, she stood, stoic and pale, in her clean dress with washed hands, facing the Elders on their dais.

Mistress Yarrow stood at her side, her hand on Hyacinth's arm as though to hold her upright. If her fingers were a little too tight, if they almost bruised, no one else would see.

"Did you hear him leave in the night, Mistress Reed?" Elder Yarrow leaned forward. They wore no masks as they stood over Hyacinth like vultures.

"I did not. I was sleeping." Her voice shook, words shuddering and falling with a clumsiness she could not steady. "I have been sleeping a lot lately due to being so unwell. I woke up with you knocking on my door. All I have now is this note of his. I have nothing left."

The bloodied piece of paper was shared between the Elders, swapped between hands. Eyes narrowed, words murmured in the hushed quiet. It was damning; Hyacinth knew that. It would damn him and spare her.

Hyacinth took a step forward, voice low. "Do you think that could be why the Teeth were so hungry? So unsated? Why the Deep came so close? Because of my husband's lust, his own appetite for flesh not belonging to his wife?"

"The sins are great," Elder Roan said, nodding slowly. "He came here carrying them through the trees when you first arrived. It would make sense that they followed. Their hunger and curiosity were piqued."

"He does not name the whore," Elder Yarrow cut in. "Have you a thought, girl?"

There was no longer a pretense of civility. Hyacinth knew he still would have more of her bones if he could. That she was doomed to be tried simply because she was not liked.

"I have met the women of this village, Elder Sir," she said, her voice calm. "I cannot imagine one of them slipping into sinful ways, not like that. I can pray for their souls and for that of my husband's and hope the hunger has been filled."

"You are the wife of an adulterer..."

"If you forgive me, Elder Yarrow," Hyacinth spoke over him, drowning out his words with her own. "I have been accused of being a witch, of bringing the Teeth and the Deep to this village, where I have only done my duty... I braved the woods with your blessing and found those lost to us. I have lost my husband and the comfort that his name and position gave me. Am I to be punished further?"

"Your future will be discussed," Elder Yarrow replied, his beady eyes dark. "We will take into account the points you have raised."

"And hang me anyway?"

"We will decide."

Hyacinth left the Drove with her mortality hanging by a thin thread. She could hardly remember a time when her life had been certain, a time when she could simply rest her head knowing she was safe. Knowing her bones were safe.

Mistress Yarrow walked beside Hyacinth, her arm linked with hers, as though they were simply escorting one another home. The silence between them stretched on, broken only when Hyacinth stepped over the threshold to her damp cottage.

"Tea?" Hyacinth asked, shaking the woman loose.

Mistress Yarrow lingered in the doorway, hesitating before closing the door behind her. She kept her distance, her hands worrying the folds of her apron. Her lovely hair was in disarray, its golden strands limp, pulled back in a greasy knot at the base of her neck.

"You could have put my name on that letter," she said, "and damned me. So many others would have."

Hyacinth put the kettle onto the burner, spooning black tea

into mugs while she waited for it to boil. "My dear husband took his life, Mistress Yarrow. I have no idea what you speak of."

"Did you drag him out by yourself? Did you wait to see if the Teeth scraped the flesh from his bones?"

Hyacinth steeped and strained the tea, adding a drop of golden honey to each mug. She passed it to Mistress Yarrow, who took it without saying a word.

"Does it matter?"

"I suppose not." She brought the tea to her lips, sipping gently. "I know he was not good to you, but he was to me. That does not make him a good man."

"Will you tell?" Hyacinth asked, the words not carrying the weight they should have.

"What good would it do?"

"It is a heavy sin to carry."

"What is one more?"

"I am not sorry that I fed him to the Teeth. I want you to know that. I am sorry to have taken him from you, though. This world is too full of fear and hunger. We consume ourselves, we starve ourselves, and the world continues to turn and feed. While I have never particularly cared for you and your smothering ways, I appreciate that you have repeatedly looked out for me. I never had intentions to hurt you."

Across the soft darkness, Mistress Yarrow's eyes shimmered. "I know. I will grieve in solitude and carry the weight of our memories always. It was enough after all these years. It was enough to know love, even for the most fleeting of moments."

Hyacinth did not know what to say, but there was a strange weight of new guilt, something small that she barely felt, but there it sat anyway.

She dreamed of Abelia again, hair alight with moonglow, eyes milk-white and wide. She danced, high up on tips toes, bones scraping the earth. And as Hyacinth watched and watched and watched, she did not ask her to dance, and she did not call to her. The soil lay damp at Hyacinth's feet, clinging to her skin as she stepped closer and followed her into the shadows, Abelia's name unspoken on her tongue. The woods were silent, too, standing still as though they were nothing but trees rooted deep. She knew better.

Hyacinth could hardly make out the path, the earth having reclaimed it. There was no one left to tame it, but her feet knew the way, her very marrow guiding her as though the map of the woods, of those roots, were carved into her soul. She found herself far in the forest, the boughs above her cluttered with yellowing bone, the strings frayed from the passing of seasons. Abelia stood in the near darkness, crouching low over the near-picked remains of Sorrell. Moss had crept over what was left of him, vines threading through the exposed cage of his ribs, tethering him down. He was as part of the woods as she.

Abelia stood, bones creaking, and outstretched her hand. She waited, lips split in an awful smile, then slipped back into the darkness.

Hyacinth awoke on the damp sofa, Faolan stretched out on top of her, weighing her down. The smell of damp wood and mold hit her senses, and the dog's warmth was not enough to keep the wet chill away. If she were not hanged or burned, then surely she would succumb to some awful damp-induced sickness taking hold of her lungs.

"Get down, you great oaf." She pushed the rough coat of Faolan from her body, and he thumped to the floor with an indignant growl. She shivered, her moist clothing unable to hold warmth. The soaked wood of the cottage had frozen, stretching the cracks wider like yawning maws. The seaweed from the Deep still clung to the eaves, the edges curling, frostbitten and sharp. She wondered if it would ever thaw or remain standing when the Deep grew angry again, pulling her cottage beneath the waves, Hyacinth and her dog within.

With dawn being some way off and the cold from the chilled walls driving through to her bones, Hyacinth stepped outside. She needed to breathe, to escape the bowing, splintered walls of her cottage and its dankness. The air was bitter, a hard frost spreading out over the ground, yet it was a dry sort of cold, and she found it tolerable. The trees around her had long shed their leaves, their boughs stripped bare, thin fingers of bark stretching out. The world around her seemed a worse place without the softness of autumn, without the greens and golds to blur the edges of everything terrible. Winter stripped it all back, forcing it naked and inescapable.

The village stood empty, everyone asleep in the remains of their homes, their doors locked fast, bones clean and ready above the doors. If any soul had once been brave enough to slip into the shadows, into the night, to meet with a friend or lover, the Teeth had forced them back. Fear and suspicion cast their safety net over those who slumbered, over those who held their sins tight, who cast accusing fingers to those, though perhaps undeserving, were easy vessels nonetheless.

Hyacinth walked alone under the pale moon. She walked past the silent, dark houses to the narrow, slippery steps that led down and down to the rocky shore. She took care, her shoes slipping on the icy stone, one hand held out to catch herself should she fall. She did not go into the woods, to the shadows that seemed to call out to her, reach for her between wakefulness and sleep. She chose the Deep over the Teeth that night.

The waves rolled in, touching the tips of her shoes, rushing over the rocks with a sigh. Moonlight dribbled down, catching the peaks and swells of the merciless waters. Hyacinth could see far, to the end of the world, she believed, if she stood on tiptoe. The wind caught her hair, forcing it from the rough knot at her nape. There, further than the Boatmen would go, she saw. Like the horrors she had glimpsed in the woods. The sight of Them stilled her heart and her lungs until she thought she would collapse from not breathing.

They rose from the depths beneath, black leviathans, eel slick and exposed bone. Abyssal Gods, awful and insatiable. She was small; the offerings made to them were small. Pitiful. They could swallow them all whole in a blink and be unmoved. As if none of them ever existed.

Hyacinth stared, her hand pressed against her chest to feel for the beating. To feel herself draw breath. She did not know if she would weep, scream, or laugh.

"It makes you think, doesn't it?"

Hyacinth startled and gasped. She turned swiftly, indignant to meet the humored gaze of Morgan.

"Were you watching me?" she demanded.

"You think mighty high of yourself, Hyacinth." He laughed, the sound too soft, too lovely. "No, I was not watching you, but them. Just think, we are here only because they wish it so. Because we humor them with our little boats and fish flesh."

"And when they grow bored?"

"I believe we have had an insight into their boredom."

"Then what is the point?"

"What would you do differently? Without the fear of the Teeth or the Deep?"

She looked out over the waves, hair in knots, skirts twisting at her ankles. "I would live unafraid, live freely."

Morgan brushed his knuckles against her hand, his skin rough. "There would always be men in skinned masks, though."

"Perhaps."

"There are old stories of boats sailing across the Deep," he began. "Old, old stories of men making the crossing on small boats piled with food and provisions, knots of carved bones, and a hamper filled with offerings, bloodied and slick."

"And how do you know they were free to cross, Mr. Carroway?"

He threaded his fingers through hers, and she allowed it. "Because some came home, Hyacinth, with wives and younguns."

"That's blasphemy."

"It is the truth."

"Aye, that's likely, too."

"There is no place for me here," Morgan said the words to the waves, voice nearly lost to the tides at their feet.

Hyacinth stood silent, eyes on the shadows far, far out into the Deep.

"It took the Boatman. It nearly dragged Sorrell to his grave." Hyacinth closed her eyes at the spray of water on her cheeks. "I saw the look on your face when you returned. You saw a nightmare that could devour worlds. You heard it sing; you said so yourself. There is nothing for you out there but a stupid death."

"I saw you drag your husband from your home the other night into the woods for the Teeth to find," Morgan said matter-of-factly.

"Then it would have been courteous of you to lend a hand," Hyacinth said without missing a beat.

"Hyacinth...."

"My father believed there could be something else out there. He did not know if it would be better—but what if there was worse? Worse than all this. What then?"

"Would you come if I asked you? Help me pack a hamper, carve the bones, and skin the flesh. Would you sit beside me and see?"

Her eyes widened. "Go across the Deep with you?"

He nodded, his other hand coming up to clasp her ruined one. With a deliberate slowness, he brought it to his lips, kissing the scars gently as though no blood had stained them.

"I'll have to bring the dog."

"You show more tenderness for that beast than anyone else," Morgan said, fingers stroking hers. "Perhaps there's some softness in there after all."

She shrugged, allowing herself to be held. To want to be held. "It took a while to carve out any softness in me," she answered, more honest than she had been in a long while. "Those easy parts to love. I carved it all out and swallowed it before the Teeth could."

"Ah," Morgan said. "Good thing I like the difficult parts. I would gladly cut myself on your sharp edges, Hyacinth."

CHAPTER TWENTY-SIX

There would be no offering of a widow's cottage for Hyacinth, given her husband's filthy sins. If they were to string her up and use her bones for her own sins, the weighty accusations clinging to her, she had yet to be told.

Hyacinth remained in her frigid cottage, yet she was seldom left alone. Packages of blankets and woolen socks, fruit-heavy crumbles, and fish soup were left on her doorstep. Tea leaves and dusty bottles of thick liquor sat beside hard bread and old cheese. At times, there were also pig feet for the dog.

The women of the village did not stop to converse with her, but they ensured she knew that, despite the bleating of the Elders, she would be cared for. In the cold darkness of her cottage, with the meager fire flickering and Morgan's offer plaguing her every thought, the simple kindness kept her warm.

She did not know what to do. What her soul would choose. She wanted to split herself into pieces so that every one of her heart-strings was content. She could admit to herself that she was afraid to stay or to go, not knowing if she would be met with Teeth or with the noose or even the flame. She wished for dominion over her ending and little more than that.

Hyacinth sat on the porch step outside her cottage with Faolan at her feet, his tail softly thumping. Her breath ghosted in front of her, the creeping cold biting through her thick cloak and the woolen mittens on her hands. It was an almost comfortable chill, grounding and calm. As near to peace as she had felt in a long, long while. In her pocket, she kept her father's fingerbone, the edges worn smooth from her rubbing. She slipped it between the cavity of her own hand, allowing it to rest there as part of her.

There was a strange quiet to the village, yet it was busier than Hyacinth could ever remember it being. Women clutched their baskets tightly as they made their way back up from the shore, cold and weary, smelling of fish and brine. They nodded to Hyacinth as they passed, reaching out to brush their hands against her. She found she missed the routine of it—of rising at dawn, curved knife in hand to skin the flesh, to watch the boats go out. To watch the early sun warm the skin on Morgan's cheeks.

Others had gathered at the forest edge, feet in the shadows, peering into the darkness beyond. Hyacinth could smell the blood on the ground, its sharpness mingling with the scent of the woods, of old bark and cold air.

"The new Woodsmen," Mistress Yarrow explained, approaching her slowly. "They were chosen last night; the hares skinned under the full moon, as is the way."

"They look so young."

"Don't they?" Mistress Yarrow plucked the wooden circlet at her neck and brought it to her lips. "May the Oaks bless them, may the Teeth spare them." She glanced to Hyacinth, lips shaping the words of prayers.

"I'll not stop you," Hyacinth said, feeling the weight of her own circlet. "If your words give heart to those children, then speak them."

"But you will not join me?"

"I will not."

Together, they watched the new Woodsmen slip beneath the boughs, the blood from their masks still gleaming. New bones were tied to their waists, enough for a circle if needed. Though the bones and the masks had not helped the former Woodsmen when the Teeth came.

"There is a meeting tonight," Mistress Yarrow informed her. "Some of us wives are gathering beforehand to weave more baskets and knit more blankets for those in need."

"I am no longer an Elder's wife, nor do I have any skills at basket weaving or knitting, as you well know. I am even less inclined to learn with so few fingers left."

Mistress Yarrow looked away, visibly uncomfortable. Whether it was because she felt sorry for Hyacinth or she felt bad she couldn't protect her, Hyacinth did not know. "Come for the company, my dear. I still need to fetch my needles and wool, and I have set out scones to cool. Mistress Roan is bringing her famous jam."

"I feel all this pity will make me fat."

"Then indulge yourself on our good graces, dear. For our souls."

Hyacinth thought of the kindness offered to her since Sorrell's death and decided it would do her well to return the favor. She followed Mistress Yarrow down the path to her cottage and watched as she dipped her head to the others they passed, sharing her prayers and well-wishes for those sent into the shadows and the Deep. They looked at Hyacinth's wounded hand and nodded back. They knew how easily it could have been them, how quickly an accusatory finger could spin to seek out blame and retribution onto those undeserving.

Candleglow seeped from the window of Mistress Yarrow's cottage as they approached, the scent of freshly baked scones drifting through the gap between the door. With her hand lingering on the door handle, Hyacinth's gaze fell upon the bones dangling over the threshold. Three of them skinned down to bones. They were barely dry, yet already they held the carving, all tied neatly with petrified wood, blackened seaweed, and shards of smooth, wave-worn glass.

"Shut the door before the heat escapes," Mistress Yarrow said, hanging up her cloak. She said nothing of the bones, of the pieces of Hyacinth strung above them. "There are fresh candles by the sink; light a few, won't you? I can't remember where I put my knitting bag."

Hyacinth did as instructed, her cold hands fumbling with the matches. "I don't know where your bag is, but I can find the scones by smell." The candle in her hand bloomed to life and joined the flickering of the lantern in the window.

"Hyacinth..."

She paused at the sound of her name.

Mistress Yarrow stood still, hand frozen on the fold of her cloak. From the shadowy eaves of the cottage, heavy footsteps crunched.

Hyacinth turned slowly, a gargle of fear bubbling from her throat.

In the darkness, beneath the beams of dried flowers and lace, it moved. The sound was not from any footfall but of *Teeth*. It carried something before it, and when it leaned forward, Hyacinth saw the wide and yellow eyes of Elder Yarrow. The thing tore through his neck with ease, sloughing the skin from his throat so Hyacinth could see the red quickness of his pulse. Threads of him dangled, all twisting veins and strips of flesh. So little holding him together.

There came a thud, and the head of Elder Yarrow cleaved free of his neck. The body, still dressed in Elder Yarrow's robes, stood swaying, severed bone jutting from the vacant space where his ugly head once sat. Then he fell slowly, slumping to the floor in an undignified heap. The Ancient stilled, long body hunched forward, shoulders shaking. Fingers folded over the graying tufts of Elder Yarrow's hair, plucking it from the floor like a fallen apple.

"Elder Lichen?"

Hyacinth recognized the torn pieces of his clothing, the thinness of him. His shoulders quaked as though he was sobbing, his fingers tight around the head, the others clawing into the wood. Then came the sound, an awful laugh that buried itself deep into every part of Hyacinth, taking root. He stood—limbs clicking, cracking, twisting—his head crooked, a smile slashed across broken lips.

Elder Lichen took a step closer, placing Elder Yarrow's head on the table with a strange sense of care. It wobbled and rolled and fell, coming to rest at Hyacinth's feet. He laughed again, mouth gaping wide, the fragile stretch of skin breaking away to reveal the bone. He stretched his arms high above his head as though simply waking from slumber, and Elder Lichen—the thing that was Elder Lichen—climbed from the flesh. Moss and seaweed hung tangled from its moldering bones, rotten sinew stretched over its antlers, trailing down over its eye sockets. It crouched low and bent, fitting its body into a space too small for something so ancient and vast.

Hyacinth had seen such a creature twice before, but it did nothing to dull the terror flooding her, blanking out her mind and seizing her senses.

The creature who had worn Elder Lichen's skin moved with a wild grace, all slowness and cracking bones, closing the scant distance between them. Hyacinth covered Mistress Yarrow with her body, her wounded hand splayed out behind her. The other fumbled around in her pockets to feel the finger bones stashed there. She retrieved one, wielding the cracked and blood-stained bone before her. She held it aloft and struck. It scraped along the curve of its collarbone, snagging on the twisted vine and tendrils of flesh. She yanked it back, pulling out its roots and tearing away its horrible screech. Claws trapped her wrist, sudden and cold. Bone against her skin, so tight she heard her own bones creak. It pulled her close, its wide open mouth releasing breath full of rot. Teeth grazed her cheek, slicing a teardrop of skin down her cheek.

"Come home."

The voice was a blasphemy; she could taste it, heavy with sin and want. She clutched the bone in her hand, feeling it break her palm. Blood slipped down her wrist, mingling with the rusted red.

"Get out of my house!" Mistress Yarrow screeched, breaking out from behind Hyacinth.

It rose, stretching higher and higher until the tips of his antlers knocked against the beams above.

"And take my fucking husband's head with you!"

With a slow bow and mouth stretched into an awful, terrible smile, it indulged her. Claw hooked around the gaping jaw of Elder Yarrow, its talons echoed through the house as it took its leave. It laughed, low and ancient and bored.

Hyacinth caught Mistress Yarrow as her knees buckled, though she did not fall. Hyacinth held her close, hand in her hair, needing the closeness as much as she.

"You did not piss yourself, Alona," Hyacinth said, noting the dryness of her skirts. "You are much braver than Sorrell ever was."

CHAPTER TWENTY-SEVEN

T hey gave Mistress Yarrow her own cottage, one on the other side of the village where the shadows of the trees slipped over the thatch. It was warm and dry, the bones newly carved and hung. The light seemed to catch it more easily, banishing the heavy darkness the old house had carried. If she feared being closer to the woods, she did not reveal it to Hyacinth. She often caught Mistress Yarrow staring out of the window, hand on the neat lace curtain, to peer past the knotted boughs.

"I can't help but think," she began, gaze locked on the woods, "that they listened to me."

Hyacinth sat at the table, the lace of the cloth draping neatly over her knees. A vase of dried flowers sat in the middle, brown husks, dead and pointless. "Who?"

"The Teeth." She came away from the window, hand going to her belly. "Since my wedding night, I prayed I would not give that man a child, and I gave him none. I prayed, my hands clasping my Oak so tight I feared it would snap. I begged the Oaks to rid me of him. I thought the drink would take him..."

"You blame yourself?"

"I credit myself, Hyacinth." She rubbed her belly again, drawing attention to the soft swell beneath her skirts. "The Oaks blessed me."

Hyacinth rose. "It is still a dreadful world to bring a child into. It is Sorrell's, then? For certain?"

"It is."

An answer to both questions, Hyacinth knew.

Mistress Yarrow was silent for a moment. When she spoke again, her words came out in the barest of whispers as though she feared the trees were listening. "Why do I feel comforted being so close? To the trees, to the shadows...the Teeth? Is my heart such a wicked thing, Hyacinth? Am I wicked?"

"You asked for your salvation, and they granted it," Hyacinth replied, leaving her cooling cup of tea on the table. She stood, laying a hand on Mistress Yarrow's shoulder. "They feast on sins and on good hearts, on who they please, when it pleases them. They taste our prayers and our confessions, our offerings, and in the end, they do as they wish. It is as simple as that."

She made to walk away but paused, hand on the door handle. "Hang your bones still, Alona, keep them carved, the lanterns lit. Stand and watch by your window, the wind on your face, and perhaps if you hear them singing, sing back."

Hyacinth left the house at the edge of the woods, and the woman within it, without a word of farewell. She passed her own crooked and bent cottage and did not look toward it. At her side, Faolan walked, his head touching her hip, feet making tracks in the frost. Down the steps she went, taking care not to slip on the frozen stone. The shore was dark and quiet, moonlight stretching out over the expanse of black water. It lay still, a mirror of the sky above.

"Are you ready?" Morgan said, outstretching a hand to her. He had pulled one of the boats up and leaned against the wood. A bag nestled within, a hamper of supplies beside it.

"It is a death of my choosing if nothing else," she replied, tossing her bag beside his.

"Your optimism is always a balm to my heart."

"And your wit to mine."

She knelt beside Faolan, taking in the way the dog trembled, how his eyes, black and wide, kept turning back to the woods, away from the Deep.

"You wildling hound," Hyacinth whispered lovingly, her words thick. She pressed her head to his, breathing in the scent of the trees, the soil, the moss, and rot. "Be gone with you! You belong out there. Go, go, Faolan!"

She shoved him away, fingers dragging through his fur.

He stilled a moment, lips curling and teeth bared, before he darted into the shadow.

Morgan's hand was cold and rough on hers, and he held it for longer than necessary, not pulling away even after she had sat and made herself comfortable. He drew her close, his fingers against her cheek, lips on hers.

The boat bobbed across the water, breaking through the pattern of stars, and when they were deep enough, the water lapping at Morgan's waist, he hauled himself in and took the oars.

She watched the shore fade away, the tall shadows of the trees growing smaller until she could barely see them. The scent of brine and winter wind filled her senses, dulling the memory of rotten wood, moss, and grass. She heard nothing but the push of water, the hot panting of her dog, and the soft grunting of Morgan as he pulled the oars.

A sail lay rumpled beneath their seats, ready to be strung up to take them further out. It was aged and yellowed, veins of black mold streaking out like branches. The Boatman seldom used them, never going far enough to hoist them up, catch the wind, and fly. She did not know how far the tattered thing would get them or if they would simply be swallowed up by the waters, oars and all.

The waves picked up as they went deeper, and Hyacinth could almost taste the promise of new beginnings. Of what lay beyond.

Morgan continued to pull the oars, pushing them farther than any boatman before them.

The wind dragged Hyacinth's hair, at her shawl, nearly tearing it free from her neck. And upon that wind, she heard it: A song, both familiar and raw, the scream of wild women. Abelia's song. Her song.

The water beneath them grew still, becoming as smooth as glass, once again reflecting the moonlight above. Morgan shifted, his knuckles white as he clutched the oars. Hyacinth dared to look over the edge, one trembling hand reaching out to the too-still water.

"Hyacinth..."

She saw them at the same time he did. Slick, oily shapes glided through the water, barely making a ripple. They seemed to take in any fraction of light until there was a nothingness Hyacinth had never encountered before. It squeezed at her, stole her breath. She could feel tendrils of something—shadow or fear she knew not—tighten around her neck.

They would not make it beyond. How foolish she was to think otherwise.

Morgan took her hands, his oars sinking, and it was that sound, the softness of the wood against the water, that nearly broke her. A quiet release.

"I would have liked to have loved you better, Hyacinth," Morgan breathed, his lips at her cheek. "For longer. I think we both deserved that."

She tasted his words, even as the boat began to sway, the pitch absolute. "I am something that is not to be endured for long."

"But you are wrong, Hyacinth."

The boat lurched, tossing Hyacinth to the floor, her knees scraping the wood. Morgan fell atop her, hands finding hers, dragging her close. Over the low, groaning cries of those below, the wild song still carried on the breeze, sharp and cold.

"We need to go back!" Hyacinth cried, her hand throbbing, the weeping mess where her fingers should have been aching. "Why did you drop the oars? We need to go back, Morgan!"

There was no light for her to see him, the stars and the moon itself swallowed by the Deep. She felt his hand touch her face more gently than ever before, and she let him.

"They are calling for you," Morgan said. "They've always been calling for you. Go!"

And he shoved her.

Hyacinth tumbled backward into the biting water, the cold sucking the breath from her. She heard the splinter of wood, the groan of the boat buckling. The waters rose, churning and screaming, hauling her under, down and down and down. Blindly, Hyacinth grappled in the waters, against the waves, desperate hands reaching. She surfaced with a scream of her own, and for a moment, she thought she had reached him, her fingers scraping flesh. She held him, fingers running over the curve of his cheek, the softness of his lip, committing his face to memory, to the part of her where Abelia dwelled. Then she let go, his head sinking far below to join the rest of him.

She was in the Deep, seaweed snaking around her ankles, blackness all around her. She stilled, waiting for the slash of teeth, of slick bodies, but nothing came.

Rocks tore at her knees as she dragged herself to the shore. The Deep took her shoes and the shawl from her shoulders, but it had left her whole. She would never know if there was anything beyond the Deep. With frozen fingers, she snatched the wooden circlet at her neck and tossed it to the waves. She offered her first prayer for Morgan, feeling tears freeze over her cheeks. Her first and only and last.

With bleeding feet and soaking skirts, Hyacinth walked through the quiet village, a place she never quite belonged, and into the woods, where perhaps she did.

Faolan waited at the edge beneath the thin, limbed trees, snow dusting his fur. His eyes were brighter than she had ever seen. He stepped beside her, his head grazing her hip, feet making no imprint on the white powdered earth.

A velveteen darkness had draped itself over everything, clinging to the boughs and branches above. There were no stars to be seen, no traces of light save for the waxy moon hanging high above Hyacinth, glowing faintly from behind heavy clouds.

Silence surrounded her, the wind having stilled, the song falling into nothingness. Her bare feet sunk through the thin blanket of snow to the dirt below, and she found herself curling her toes to sink them deeper and feel for the roots. The cold slipped away as she walked, the air smelling of the familiar decay, and she found herself breathing deeply, drawing into her lungs.

From the shadows, Abelia stepped, all pale limbs and knotted hair. She walked closer, feet shuffling with that strange grace. From behind her, the creature that had been Elder Lichen stood, towering over them both, stretching up into the trees, his antlers scraping the clouds. One clawed hand curled over Abelia, but he looked down to Hyacinth, his maw gaping wide, ropes of ivy and weeds dripping from teeth and bone. He laughed, and the sound was the song of the trees of the dark, of wickedness.

It was terrible and lovely, and she found herself laughing too.

"Welcome home, Hyacinth," Abelia said, mouth to hers, breathing moss sweet. Her hands, pale and cold, reached into her hair, drawing Hyacinth closer. Her lips grazed over her cheek, tongue tasting the teardrops that slipped until there were no more.

"Welcome home."

ACKNOWLEDGMENTS

It is hard to believe that this book started life as a cozy cottage-core mystery, though it wasn't long before the need to turn things darker and blooder began to take over. I have Chesney Infalt to thank for that, for being supportive of my attempt at something soft, but also not holding back her glee when I wanted torn flesh and bone. You were the first to see the horror take shape, and I do hope it is awful enough for you.

Thank you to Cassandra for seeing the dreadful potential in *The Bone Drenched Woods*. Working with you on this book has been the best ride, you have helped Hyacinth become fiercer, more determined, more herself than I could have hoped for. I enjoyed plotting ways with you to bring more horror, terror, blood, and bone into these pages. You know my voice, and I will always be thankful for that.

(Thanks to all the wonderful editors here, I love you!)

And of course, my unending thanks to my wonderful husband, for the writing snacks and the endless cups of tea and coffee. And for the fabulous clicky clacky keyboard that drives you mad.

My writing will always be for my girls, my imps. You are yet too young to enjoy horror, but I do live in hope. Stay weird and wonderful.

ABOUT THE AUTHOR

 L.V. Russell grew up in a haunted cottage deep in the Dorset countryside alongside her three elder brothers, using the fields and woodland as their playground. As an adult with two young children, she has used the memories of the wild woods of her youth to write stories about faeries and ghosts and the old whispering oaks. When she is not writing, she is most likely to be found exploring the woods near her home, or curled up by candle-light with a good book.

Also by L.V. Russell
The Quiet Stillness of Empty Houses

THANK YOU FOR READING

Thank you for reading *The Bone Drenched Woods.* We deeply appreciate our readers, and are grateful for everyone who takes the time to leave us a review. If you're interested, please visit our website to find review links. Your reviews help small presses and indie authors thrive, and we appreciate your support.

More Books from Quill & Crow

The Quiet Stillness of Empty Houses, L.V. Russell

There Ought to Be Shadows, Krissie K. Williams

The Secrets of Blackthorn House, Marie McWilliams